AN M-Y BOOKS HARDBACK

© Copyright 2009
Roger Slater

The right of John Slater to be identified as the
author of
this work has been asserted by him in accordance
with the
Copyright, Designs and Patents Act 1988

A CIP catalogue record for this title is
available from the British Library

ISBN 9781906986711

GW00537738

Published by
M-Y Books
www.m-ybooks.co.uk

Hertford uk

Front cover by M-Y Books Design

THE STORIES

OF

JOHN SLATER

Contents

<u>DEDICATION.</u>

"To the two women in my life: My mother for keeping the stories safe and my wife for supporting me in this endeavour."

THE LORD RIX Kt CBE DL

<u>FOREWORD by Brian Rix</u>

I first met John Slater in 1951. I had just joined the Stage Cricket Club and I had a car! Johnnie was the very first passenger/player I picked up. As he came out of the house he looked more like a Romany than an already well-known actor, with his mop of black curly hair and a red 'kerchief tied round his neck, and I suspect he would have been quite happy adopting that lifestyle, for he was an extraordinarily gifted extrovert who was prepared to explore all forms of theatre - from farce to tragedy - who loved touring and the opportunities it gave him to play hundreds of rounds of golf - was mad on cricket and was both a hard-hitting middle order batsman and a more than useful wicket-keeper and was a wonderful friend to both Elspet and me at the lowest point of our lives when our first child, Shelley, was born with Down's Syndrome. The only handicap he seemed to have was a dicky heart and despite an early valve replacement -

which he chose to ignore despite its loud clicking - it was this that killed him after an emphatic farewell on BBC telly, playing Det. Sgt. Stone in the ground-breaking police series - Z Cars.

His fame on television had come much earlier, though, when the BBC was the only show in town. John won one of the first awards for the wonderful short stories he wrote and presented on both radio and television and I believe this book will give many readers the answer why he was so successful. Of course, without John's craggy face to accompany them, they have to stand on their own feet. And they do! Because I know the family so well I think I like the opening story "The Long Voyage Home" most of all. The bravery of both John and Betty is underplayed in this saga - but I wonder how many people know that John was filmed in "A Passport to Pimlico" with his broken leg always hidden from the camera or that Betty was one of Archie McIndoe's "guinea pigs" at East Grinstead - and the only woman, to boot. Throughout the years he was with me in "Reluctant Heroes" and "Dry Rot" I noticed the bright red skin on Johnnie's left hand as a visible sign of that horrendous crash but I never recall the memory of it clouding his wonderful performances or, most precious of all, his friendship.

I could go on ... and on ... but this foreword is in danger of turning into a short story in its own right. Let me finish by saying I trust the thousands of viewers who remember John - probably all now well on in years - will buy this work, for it is ideal bedtime or travel time reading. But younger readers should give it a go too, for as John's son, Roger, has said in his introduction these stories "will bring pleasure to all who enjoy being transported to another place."

And that is all of us, surely.

AN INTRODUCTION BY Roger Slater

In 1946 my parents took a delayed honeymoon in France. On the return flight the plane crashed, killing twenty-one people.

My father had some sort premonition and did not fasten his seat belt. When the plane crashed he was blown out of the side. He returned to the burning wreck and was carrying my mother clear when the plane blew up. A piece of metal went through his left leg, breaking the bone.

He always used to say that what gave him the strength to save them, both was the Steak Tartare he had had before take-off. True or not, the fact remains that he went on to become one of the most versatile British actors of the 20th century, appearing in diverse productions of Shakespeare, Pinter, Miller, Osborne, Pinky & Perky, several Whitehall Farces and a host of films. Towards the end of his life he became a household name as the fearsome Sergeant Stone, in the television series 'Z Cars', but a generation earlier he won an Oscar as the 'Television Actor of the Year' for series such as 'Eight to a Bar' and 'Johnny You're Wanted', and for his telling of stories. As well as telling stories on television he also wrote them for the radio and for magazines. They are stories of a gentler age. They lack the violence, cruelty and sex of many, more modern tales, but will bring pleasure to all who enjoy being transported to another place. Millions enjoyed them in their first incarnation, this is your chance to enjoy them again - if you're old enough - or for the first time, if not.

The first story is actually his account of their return journey from France, many months after the crash.

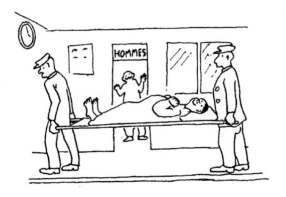

THE LONG VOYAGE HOME: 1/10/'46

"Take a couple of pills, eh?" said the Sister; "You've got a long day tomorrow."

And so tomorrow began, reluctantly, with a long swim up to the surface of consciousness, goaded by a thermometer.

The first hours of the morning - six to nine-thirty - passed like a prolonged sigh. A relieved one perhaps, from the staff, for I am not a good patient; and a sad one from my fellow patients for, after all, it is good to listen to someone saying all the things that you wanted to say yourself, but didn't dare. A sort of clinical 'Counsel for the Defence'.

Then the moving started: "Lift - shift - whoa. Lift - shift - whoa." (Shades of a BBC early morning exercise programme) Still, it gets me onto the stretcher and the first part of the journey begins with a roll down the corridor to the lift, then carried by a team of acrobats up some stairs, round some corridors, down some stairs and into the ambulance. Acrobats, because no matter what angles of incline, decline, incidence, or for that matter coincidence, were encountered, I remained flat; while they, at times, resolved into corkscrews!

Betty followed soon after, quiet and white, whiter for the broad bandage round her forehead, covering the only remaining burn (on her face); she looks like a doll that some little girl has been playing 'hospitals' with, and in truth she is little more - drugged, plastered: only her eyes move. Sometimes they smile at me.

Now the nurses. Betty's favourite nurse, suspiciously moist-eyed, kisses her goodbye. My favourite nurse, just suspicious, shakes my hand - maybe it was a mistake to grow this beard - oh well.

My father-in-law gets in. The nurse from London gets in. The doors slam. Half a mile down the road we realise that we have neither this nor that and, as we shall undoubtedly have need of both of them before we reach London, the driver gets down and runs back - a procedure quite obviously quicker than trying to turn an ambulance on a French main road.

About twenty minutes later, puffed but triumphant, he is back at a jog-trot, to a clanging that clearly announces the contents of his white-wrapped bundle, and we are away again.

There follows the inevitable hootings, breakings, "salauds!" of a drive across Paris. Through the slit of a window I can see the little blue and white street names high up on buildings, and report on our progress towards the Gare du Nord; and before my periodic "just a few minutes now" can become an admission of ignorance, I recognise the Madeleine, and it truly is 'just a few minutes'.

Really, this is the way to travel! The manager of the Southern Railway, the station master, the assistant station master, and the Consular office are there to smooth out the technicalities. The R.A.M.C. is there to smooth out the stretcher-bearing and the British amateur wrestling team is there with a bottle of champagne.

The boys take Betty first - "it's my legs that are so heavy" she says.

"Lassie," says the sergeant," if they were set in all the plaster in Paris you'd still be the lightest load I've ever handled" - and the nervous tear in the corner of her eye twinkled in the sun, but did not fall.

I felt good! I felt wonderful! This was the way to travel and these were the boys to get you cracking. I dug into my blankets and found the half-bottle of gin with half an inch left in the bottom by some kind friend, for just such an occasion, and I toasted them all; the S.R., The S.M., the A.S.M., the Consulate, the army and Paris - I toasted all of them in one uvula-jerking mouthful.

And then they were back for me. Up, off and into the steady, rhythmic, practised pace of the professional - something like riding a camel flat on your back. Yes! This is the way to travel. Straight through the barrier, straight through the crowd, straight up the platform. Still, I suppose that they know where they're going: straight..... straight ......?

Shades of 40 hommes and 8 chevaux! The meat van? What the -?

> "Voyez m'sieur, il est impossible."
> "Sorry old man, but we couldn't..."
> "...à mettre les brancards ..."
> "... get the stretchers ..."
> "... par les fenêtres ..."
> "... through the windows ..."

So, with French and English explanations and apologies spattering through the roar of the engine, ten feet away, like a hose pipe playing on Niagara, we are stowed into the meat van. What's more, we are strung by cords to the meat rail; to prevent, we are told, the stretchers running up and down the van with the motion of the train.

Some motion! Never before have I noticed that a train progresses by rapid sideways leaps, like an exhilarated crab or by forward bounds, like a kangaroo with hiccups. The windows, wired and grilled, are closed; but through the gaps around the big metal sliding doors, through the brown paper stuffed into the gaps, whistles the wind, like a maniac with a tar brush, coating us and everything that is ours with a layer of soot.

Betty is very white now. Her pallor is phosphorescent through the soot. At her feet the nurse sits on the boards trying to steady the rolling of her plastered legs. You can't do much when every sleeper seems to deliver its own separate, vindictive punch through the floor. But she is trying, bless her, and for four hours she went on trying.

At Amiens the train stops. A nurse heads a flurry of officials - come to see if the meat's cold, I suppose unhappily, and I ask for a sandwich. Somebody brings a snooker cue and a bottle of Evian water and off we go again, with me feeling somewhat annoyed about the cue, until I find that it has a core of sausage and is delicious. Trouble is, it takes so long to eat that soon the grey French bread is black and grit fills my teeth like currant pips - it's even in the

- 16 -

Evian water, so I have to suck that in jets, using the space between my front teeth as a strainer.

Maybe it is the effect of a full stomach or maybe garlic is an anæsthetic, but anyway, soon I am asleep, to wake up as we are drawing into Calais.

We are boarded by a young and enthusiastic Customs Officer:
"Anything to declare, Madame?" to the nurse.
One thousand, three hundred francs and a bottle of lavender water belonging to Betty."
"Bien, et vous, m'sieur?" to me.
"One broken leg, one burned leg, two burned hands, a beard, some plaster of Paris and a bottle of champagne." - I am feeling neither young or enthusiastic! He went.

Silly of me really. He was probably quite a nice chap and would have stayed and chatted with me while the army are once again dealing with Betty. But very soon they are back for me and very gently they slide me out. So this is what a side of beef feels like. Or, more accurately, a smoked, not to say singed, ham. But this is pleasant. This is progress. A glimpse of water as we go up the gang-plank and suddenly I know that the bridge from the past to the future is about three feet wide, twenty feet long and slopes up from Calais to 'The Canterbury'.

The steward recognises me - the last time we met I was on my way to Rome. The purser comes in to the alcove that has been curtained off for us, to assure us of a mill-pond crossing. Betty is still dubious but he soothes her and adds "We have the worst behind us now, haven't we? And we must draw comfort from our miraculous escape, mustn't we?"

Which I heartily endorse, and while unacquainted with any particular catastrophe from which he himself has escaped, I am very glad that he did so, as he is a comfortable and kind man, and we drink his health in the champagne which has survived the meat van remarkably well. Betty and I eat tongue sandwiches with the champagne and it gives us an exotic feeling, like going to Tibet for a picnic. And when Betty asks, "When do we leave?" we are delighted to tell her that we left twenty minutes ago. To prove it I heave up my leg, sit on my pillows, look out of the window and report "nothing but sea in sight, and very unexciting sea it is too."

Not so unexciting was the sight of my father and brother-in-law, who seemed to be trying to throw themselves off the dockside as we edge in. Luckily we get close enough for them to have a better view from where they are than from the water, and we mouth excited greetings at each other until they are allowed on board.

Betty is first away again and I light a cigarette and sing - somewhat plaintively - "J'attendrai", to the accompaniment, from the next compartment, of a female American voice singing, equally plaintively, for a porter. She gets a porter before the porters get me, and calls a friendly "Good luck," as she goes by and rolls a startled eye when I say "The same to you". "J'attendrai" and a beard don't go with English as she is spoke.

Soon they come for me and up on the deck my lungs inflate properly for the first time in a month. The air has a quality of life, an edge on it. I suck it from the bosom of the sea, from the dockyards, from the cliffs and the grass that crowns them. From England.

Somewhat apprehensive, I find myself being loaded into a luggage van; but the luggage van leads in to a state room, carpeted and armchaired. Our two new members are unpacking tea, cocoa, chicken soup, fruit and sandwiches. Betty lies in morphined quiet in the corner. The nurse still sits beside her - on the floor.

The journey is lost in food and drink and soft conversation. Night paints the windows blue and they lift me a little to see the beginning of London flicker past.

Tenderly we settle into Victoria - can you imagine, a train, tenderly? - but that's the word, believe me; and more anxious, loving faces are at the window. But Betty is awake now and this is too much. Too much of sweetness too soon on too much of sorrow. So no-one moves.

This time they take me first - the four men of Daimler - and fit me onto the stretcher that fits their car. As they blanket me and strap me I feel the first rain, and lightning whips the cover of darkness off the blitzed roof long enough for me to see a policeman standing close by.

> "Whose side you on sarge?"
> "Don't worry mate, I'm on yours."

Well, there's a first time for everything!

The platform is clear and again I am swung off in professional rhythm. If their ambulance is as good as they are then ... Surely this isn't it? This long, high, black..... 'Oh now put out the light, we come to bury Slater not to'.... but they put on the light instead and I see that inside, the ominous body is warm and brown, albeit slightly surgical in the chromed efficiency of the stretcher-rest which swings out to receive me and flips back with me on it, like a fly on a lizard's tongue.

I hold brief court with the welcoming party, then Mother and Father get in and sleekly, noiselessly we move off.

This is luxury; this is comfort undreamed of. When I am very rich I shall buy one of these and travel no other way. The very traffic lights blush and then turn green with envy, and we proceed urbanely. Marble Arch; Baker Street; St. John's Wood; Swiss Cottage; the lovely names that roll off the glistening road like pearls off a broken string. Golders Green; Henley's Corner - we're going home! We're going to pass the top of my road! "Can't we stop at the 'Malt and Hops' and get a pint?" Past Finchley Central. Past Tally-Ho Corner. Past the 'Malt and Hops' - really, it wouldn't have hurt me, a pint.

North we go, through Barnet, and further North. Lightning shows a corner and a low semi-circular building. We drive in and unload. Swing doors yammer behind me.

"This is your room Mr Slater."
Lift - shift - whoa. Lift - shift - whoa.
"There, are you comfy?"

Comfy? To be cradled in a cloud, pillowed on powder-puffs and covered with cloth-of-gold. Comfy?!

WHAT'S IN A GRAVE?

The other day, after I'd finished work, I went over the road for a drink and a game of darts with Jackie from the fish shop. And we were picking our way through a nice steady 301 up, when a feller moves across from the bar and asks if he can take chalks - that means that he scores for us, then plays the winner.

"O.K." I said, and as I put the chalk in his hand I saw that it was like the rest of him, square and heavy - but sort of gentle - like a man who could write poetry with a pick-axe. He was a bloke of about fifty-five, and I hadn't seen him in these parts before. So, "O.K.", I said, and when I had finished off Jackie I took him on.

It was a whitewash. I didn't even get started. He knocked off 301 in fourteen darts, finishing with a double top.

"Well," I said, "very neat. Mr..... Mr. ...er?"
"Ripp" he said, "Charlie Ripp."

"Rip", says Jackie, "How do you spell it, R.I.P.?
Must be a dead and alive kind of existence!"

"Please," he said. "Please, I have heard most of
the jokes before - pint of bitter, please - as a
matter of fact it used to be spelt R.I.P., but I
decided to change it very early on in my life.
You see, in the village where I was born, the
school was on the other side of the churchyard:
Village; Churchyard; School. There was a way
round the churchyard of course, but I was
about the only one who ever used it, and that
was only because I got sick of the other kids
dancing round me and singing things like "Old
Charlie R.I.P. six feet under and can't catch
me!" The fact that my father was the local
stonemason, and did all the inscriptions didn't
help much either. By the time that I was
thirteen or so I was getting really sensitive
about it - it's a sensitive time for a young fellow
anyway, you know, when he starts putting sticky
stuff on his hair and realises that girls aren't
just something his mother wishes he was. I
remember how I lost my first girl: I was
walking her home through the churchyard, when
one of her friends goes by and says 'Pick
yourself a nice place to stay, Elsie; They say his
father's already carving out the invitations, in
Marble!'
She never spoke to me again after that.
Wouldn't even let me carry her books. And it

was always the same, no girl would even look at me, even my pals used to pull my leg about it and it got so that I used to feel hunted and persecuted. In the end, I made up my mind that I'd change my name - nothing serious, just start spelling it differently - R.I.P.P., instead of R.I.P.

It was the end of term, so the first chance I got of doing it was on my examination papers; and the first paper we got was English Composition. I was always good at that - you know, making things up - in fact I always used to get enough marks on my English paper to make up for the marks I didn't get on my Maths paper. Well, I wrote a good composition and when I signed it at the bottom 'Charles Ripp, 'R.I.P.P.', I felt happy for the first time in weeks.

Until the next day when I got the paper back. The only note was right at the end: old Brooksey, he was the English teacher, had drawn a line right through the second 'P' I'd added to the R.I.P. and in red ink he'd written "I observe that you are no longer able to write your own name." And under that he'd written "Nought out of Ten." I felt like a handful of wet earth.
Brooksey wasn't interested when I went to him and told him what was worrying me. "R.I.P. -

R.I.P.P.- Nonsense boy! What's in a name? A rose by any other name smells just as sweet."

I tried to explain to him that it wasn't a question of smelling but spelling. "Your patronymic, boy, should be your proudest possession. It marks your place. Your estate."

"Yes," I said, "six feet of earth.

But he wouldn't wear it and I had a terrible time explaining my marks to my dad. And when he found out the truth, he didn't half give me what for.

Changed the whole course of my life that did. After the war I didn't go back home. I changed my name to R.I.P.P. and followed the trade in London. Only went back to the village to see my father just before he died.

I've got my own business now, just the other side of Islington, where you'll get as good a bit of stone masonry as you'll find anywhere in England - if you gentlemen should be thinking ahead a bit.

And I'd never have gone back to the village again if I hadn't had a letter, about a year ago, from, of all people, old Brooksey - he was still there - telling me that they planned to have a school reunion to celebrate the opening of a new school hall. I didn't answer, but funny enough, when the time came, I went. I don't know why. I suppose that at my time of life yesterday's a happier day to spend than tomorrow. And I must say, when I got there, I enjoyed it. There were some changes, of course. Two wars, income tax and a few epidemics had thinned us out a bit, like long hair across a bald spot, but the biggest shock was that old Brooksey had died a couple of weeks after he wrote to us all.

"Do you remember" I said to Elsie, "that time when he gave me nought out of ten, for signing myself R.I.P.P. instead of R.I.P."

She smiled and took forty years off her face. "Oh yes, and do you remember ...."

"What didn't we remember that night, all of us. When the party was over, we even remembered the way back to the village from the school, through the churchyard. Which was just as well, 'cause it was quite a party. Not that anybody said or did anything out of place. That is, until we decided to walk back through the churchyard.

In the moonlight, it looked like a mouthful of broken teeth, and we walked quite quietly along the little path until one of the fellers - maybe he'd had a drop more than he could handle - tripped over a stone that was jutting out a bit. When he picked himself up he looked at the headstone, which was standing out clear under the moon: "I might have known it!" He said. "Old Charlie up to his tricks again."

We all looked and we saw that the headstone had nothing on it except 'R.I.P.' cut big and sharp into the marble. And then they started:

"Here you are Charlie, home from home."
"Hop in Charlie, room for one more inside."

They even sang the 'Can't catch me' song. And me, I felt like a kid again. I could have burst out crying, there in the churchyard. Then I got angry. I took out a fine chisel that I always carry around in a little leather case, picked up a stone and tapped out another 'P', so now it really read "R.I.P.P." "There you are", I said, "Now perhaps you're all satisfied. Underground. That's where you want me, and that's where I am as far as the lot of you are concerned from now on!"

About four o'clock the next morning I woke with a horrible feeling; it wasn't all hangover; I felt that something terrible had happened.

Then I remembered. And I couldn't believe it. Maybe it was a nightmare, brought on by that old unhappiness. But me! Desecrate a tombstone. In my business. Well, it would finish me in the trade if it ever got out. I stuffed my night-shirt into my trousers and rushed down the empty village street. The moon was still bright and when I got to the churchyard it didn't take me long to spot that bright, new headstone. I came up to it very slowly; I could soon see the deep cut 'R.I.P.', then, as I got closer, I saw that there was a second 'P', fresh cut, alongside. I'd really done it. I must have been mad. I walked right up to it, to see if there was anything I could do quickly to wipe it out. And as I got right near to the stone I suddenly saw that there was a line drawn right through that second 'P', and underneath it, '0/10'. "

THE WIG

This is a wig that isn't a wig. At least, *I've* never worn it. The last person who did wear it gave it to me as a good luck charm, and I've kept it as such ever since.

It was when I worked in a circus once, years ago. There weren't any other jobs around, and rather than be out of work over Christmas I took a job as one of those handy men around the place - you know, the ones who come flying into the circus ring and tidy up when the clowns or the elephants or the other various acts have done their bit and the next act is waiting to come on.

Well, the star attraction of this particular circus was a 'high-wire' act, called "The Highwaymen". They were four brothers and their sister and they used to dress up like a bunch of Dick Turpins and carry off the girl, kicking and screaming, all along the high-wire strung right across the big top.

It was a wonderful act - used to scare me to death every night - and this was in the days before the law said that high-wire acts had to work with a safety net. The Highwaymen, Dave, Joe, Harry and Ben went sliding around up there like they were strolling down Regent Street; slinging Marie, their sister, around like a basket ball. It all seemed so easy and they looked really smart in their neat black periwigs, three-cornered hats, ruffles and riding coats.

Three of the wigs were black, but Dave, he was the eldest brother, always wore this white one. He was quite a bit older than the others and the boss of the outfit. In fact, it was his last Christmas on the high-wire. We got quite pally as time went by and he told me he reckoned that his time was up. "Get out Johnny," he said to me. "Get out before you fall out. That's what my father used to say."

"He was on the wire, was he?" I asked.

"Oh yes. Dad started the act. He and mamma and me and then when Marie grew up she took over from mamma, so that mamma could look after the family."

"I see" I said, "Then you took over when your father gave up. You put on the white wig. Is that the custom, for the leader of the troupe to wear a white wig?"

"Well," he said, "not exactly, though this is my father's wig; in fact, it's his hair. - Oh don't worry," he laughed, "I didn't scalp him. All our wigs are made that way; we grow our hair long and keep on saving the pieces that are cut off. Then, when we've got enough, we have wigs made of our own hair and then walk around looking normal when were not on the wire."

"Long way round of doing it, isn't it?" I said.

"I don't know Johnny," he said, "all the best wigs are made of human hair you know, and it's just our tradition to use our own."

"I see," I said, "and you use your father's to this day. The white one."

"Yes, that's right. The white one. I'll give it to you for luck when the season's over."

"You're joking!" I said. "It's a very generous thought, but I couldn't take it, I wouldn't want to break your luck."

"Don't worry, I won't need that sort of luck anymore. My father would be happy to know that some young man just making his way was carrying it with him. You see the first time that I wore it, I was just making my way. The first time that I led the troupe I wore my father's wig. My father didn't give up like I am giving up. He didn't want to give up, but we made him. For months mother and I, and the others, argued and argued with him."

"Poppa please" mamma used to say, "enough is enough; you've earned your rest; why don't you take it?"

"You mean I'm too old" he said. "The old horse must go into the field and eat and sleep until he dies?"

"No poppa," we said, "of course we don't mean that. Nobody can take your place."

"Then why do you want me to give up?'"

"Well, there's Harry and Ben. They're grown up now, they want to come into the act and work."

"They're learning aren't they? I'm teaching them, aren't I? I'll know when they're ready; and I'll tell them. Nobody tells me!"

And that's how it went on for months. Everybody bad tempered with everybody else. Harry and Ben swearing that they would run away and start an act of their own and take Marie with them. That made father more furious than anything. Marie was the apple of his eye, and that brought the real reason for his refusal to give up right out into the open: "If you think I would trust little Marie to a bunch of clumsy, ham-fisted, flat-footed layabouts, you're all crazy. I would tear down the wire with my bare hands before she should put a foot on it without me there. When the time comes I will tell you. And it will come when I say so, not before!"

I know that I'm making poppa sound like the villain of the piece, aren't I? A real old tyrant. But he wasn't, believe me he wasn't. It was only because he loved us all so, that he was afraid for us. Perhaps more afraid for Marie than for the rest of us because she had spent all her life trusting him, only him. And up there on the wire he handled her like a doll; a precious china doll that walked and talked and looked only at his command. His was always the hand, the voice that guided her. His were always the arms that carried her off. He would never trust her even to me.

For all that, however, the time for us youngsters to take over the act came sooner than he thought. And it wasn't the high-wire, that thin thread of danger, that broke him - it was the doctors.

"Dave" they said, "your poppa must stop. His heart is no good anymore - he is a danger to you and to himself. If he carries on up there on the wire, we won't be responsible for what may happen."

And this they left *me* to tell him. Can you imagine how I felt? Standing there in our practice clothes, saying to this great little man, with muscles braided like a young girl's hair, his bright eyes and his thick black, brilliant black, hair - saying to him, "poppa, the doctors say you must stop now."

I don't know what I expected to happen. But nothing did.

"I know son," he said. "I know. Doctors don't have to tell me, you don't have to tell me. These things a man knows for himself. It's not fair anymore for any of you to have me up there with you on the high-wire. But you cannot go on yet, any of you, without me. You're not ready; this too I know, and better than you."

"Then what do we do, poppa?" I said.

"Why are you worried?" he said. "It's simple. I stop, we stop."

"But poppa...."

"Wait" he said, "wait. Patience - that's all we need - a little patience. We will cancel our contracts, and we will practice. We will practice until little Marie is as safe with you as if I was still up there with you. And then the Highwaymen will come back to the high-wire even better than we ever were."

"Poppa", I said, "that's wonderful. But we'll never be as good without you."

"Rubbish!" he said. "Rubbish, is that the way to talk? You'll be better - You'll have to be better before Marie treads the wire with you!"

And as he said we would do, so we did. We practised 'till our feet were sore; until our toes could play the wire like a guitar; until our arms were heavy and our clothes and our bright black wigs were wet with sweat.

We practised in a great barn all through the summer, with a tight safety-net below us and the big Christmas circus in London waiting for us.

And then one day, when the Autumn night was already beginning to shadow the barn, poppa said "Right. My children you are ready."

And the next day, there in the barn, Harry and Ben and I put on our black wigs and our highwaymen's clothes and we practised the act right through. And there was no net.

The dress rehearsal went without a hitch and we all had a glass of champagne when it was over. "Now" said poppa, "now we have something to show London. To you, all my darlings," and he lifted his glass, "To the Highwaymen!"

So he toasted us and wished us well. But he never saw us. In those last few weeks before the circus began in London, he suddenly became an old man. He seemed to shrink before our eyes and his hair was a dusty grey against his bright black wig that stood on the block in front of his mirror.

It was half an hour before the first performance that the new Highwaymen were to give, when the manager came to our dressing room and said "Dave". He couldn't say any more, but I knew:

"Poppa", I said.

"Yes", he said, "it's your father. He's in my office. The doctor came right away, but he was too late."

"Poppa's gone," I said.

"Yes, Dave." He's gone. "His last words were 'Tell Dave everything's all right, just look after little Marie.' I'll announce that you can't go on."

"No you won't," I said. "We'll go on; that's what poppa would have wanted."

"All right Dave," he said, "if you say so."

And so we got dressed. None of us said anything and it wasn't until our call came and I started to get my wig on that I realised that it wasn't mine - we'd brought poppa's wig by mistake, but after a moment it felt right, and I felt glad that I was wearing it; shiny and black, the way we remembered his hair.

Up there on the high-wire the world seemed to dwindle away into a little sea of faces below us, and the act went better than ever we had rehearsed it, until the very last run. Marie was running away from me across the wire, when I saw her slip. As she fell I threw myself towards her, locking a foot grip on the wire as I went, and I caught her by the ankle as she was dropping. We hung there until the net was up below us. It seemed like forever but it couldn't have been more than a moment, and then we dropped safely into it, and all the time I could hear poppa saying "Look after little Marie."

We went up again right away and finished the act; This you must always do or you'll never get your nerve back.

And I was surprised, as we bowed to the audience, that I felt nothing. I could have been taking a walk in the park. And it wasn't until I got back to the dressing room that I saw that my wig - poppa's bright, black wig - was white now.

DEAR THOMAS

Have you ever had one of those Christmases when you all sit round telling creepy stories? It's fun, but you have to watch it: sometimes you can get more creep than Christmas.

Take us last year: Christmas eve it was, the kids were in bed, Bert and Elsie from next door had left their Michael watching Telly and popped in for a drink - well he was fourteen and he wanted to watch the James Bond Film - and we were all in our living room with a glass full of this or that and stomachs full of pre-Christmas stuffing. And Mrs Moore was with us.

Mrs Moore is our 'daily' and she'd been working for us for about six months then. A quiet, gentle little woman she was and we didn't know much about her except that she seemed to be a lonely soul; so when the wife suggested we invite her to spend Christmas with us and give a hand around the place, I thought it was a good idea - especially when I thought about how much less washing up I would have to do!

It didn't take long, of course, what with the warmth of the flickering fire, the lights on the tinselled tree and the drink, for us to get round to yarning. I kicked off with that beauty about the girl who rushes up to a bloke and screams that she's just seen a feller with no face, in the churchyard, and he turns to her and says "What, like mine?"! Then everybody had a go, and eventually we came to Mrs Moore.

"Come on Mrs Moore," I said, "You know the formula, something creepy for Christmas."

"Oh no sir," she said, "I don't know any stories."

"Go on," I said, "I bet you know as many as that Arabian Princess. Let's see if another Port and Lemon will help you remember." And the others joined in, chivvying her to tell us a tale, while I went round and filled up all the glasses. "Now then Mrs Moore," I said as I sat down, "Let's hear from you."

"Well.... oh I don't know.... it's silly.... well: Just after the war my married daughter was living with me. Her husband didn't come back you see, and after her little boy was born in December, she didn't seem to have any will to live any more. 'Mum' she said, 'call him Tom.' So I was left with the little chap. Now, at the time I was working for some lovely people, called Jamieson;

high up civil servant he was - Post Office, or BBC. I think he was, something to do with licences anyway - They really were a nice couple; not very old but they'd been married for ten years or so and were ever so much in love. It broke their heart that they couldn't have any children, and they made a proper fool of their cat. Thomas his name was, 'Dear Thomas' they always called him. Mark you, as cats go, he was a smasher - he was the biggest cat I've ever seen, black as your hat, he didn't walk, he poured himself out, like a glass of stout. Lived like a lord he did; even had his own china, and a bed that swung gently when he got into it, to rock him off to sleep. He had most of his meals sitting between them at the table and when I took them up their morning cuppa', he was usually curled up on the bottom of the bed, and he always had his saucer of tea first.

Well, of course, after little Tom was born I had to have him with me all the time. He was as good as gold in the pram, but he only had to open his mouth to yawn and Mrs Jamieson'd have him up in her arms fussing over him, and if he cried I could hardly keep her out of Harley Street. So in a way I wasn't surprised when Mr Jamieson asked if he could have a chat with me: 'Mrs Moore,' he said, 'you doubtless know that ... ahem ... you are probably aware of ...

that is ... you must have realised ... Mrs Moore, you know we cannot have any children of our own, may we adopt young Tom?'

Well, what could I say? I loved him, but I wasn't his mother, and I was getting on a bit. Besides, look what they could do for him. And they said that I could go on working for them until Mr Jamieson got shifted somewhere by the Ministry, so I'd be with him. It took quite a while for everything to be arranged, but in the end my Tom became Tom Jamieson.

The only one who wasn't so happy about all this was Dear Thomas. But after a few months even he got used to the idea and then, it was ever so funny, he went the other way, he stuck to Tom like a shadow: sat by his highchair; slept on a nursing stool by his cot; went shopping in the pram with him; played with his beads and teething toys; walked down the garden with him, with his big, amber eyes blinking at the birds as if to say 'just you come near him, and see what I'll do to you.'

They were the talk of the neighbourhood. Some thought it was sweet; some thought it was amusing and some thought it was unhygienic. But none of it made any difference, they were together and that was that.

Then one day, when Tom was about four years old, a terrible thing happened: he'd been naughty, very naughty, as boys that age will be, and Mrs Jamieson smacked him, and before you could say 'knife' Dear Thomas flew at her; all black, bristling fur and claws, with eyes like red-hot coals. Luckily, I was in the kitchen, just taking some washing out of the machine, so I had him off her and wrapped in a wet towel before he did any real damage. But when Mr Jamieson came home that evening they talked it over, during dinner, and when I came in to clear away he said 'Mrs Moore, we have decided that Thomas must go.'

'Go sir?'

'Yes. Young Tom is getting a big boy now. He's at an age when boys must begin to learn what is wrong and what is right. Inevitably that means that occasionally he will have to be punished and in this we cannot be dictated to by Thomas. So Thomas must go.'

'Where sir?'

We shall take him to.... to the vet, tomorrow evening, when I return from the office. Please see that his travelling basket is ready, will you?'

They were nearly in tears, the pair of 'em. And so was I for that matter.

Late the following afternoon they set off, with Thomas curled up, half asleep, in his basket. The late sun made the day's earlier rain glisten, like teardrops. I tell you straight, I cried like a child, and I sent Tom off to play in the nursery.

They were back inside the hour. The basket was empty. 'Where's Tom,' they asked.

'In the nursery,' I replied.

They went upstairs, but in a few minutes they were back. 'He's not there,' said Mrs Jamieson.

'Oh well,' I said, 'he's probably playing somewhere round the house.' And I went with them to look.

We looked everywhere. In every room, out of every window, on every floor, calling 'Tom, Tom,' as we went. By the time we got to the top, front attic we were beginning to get worried. Then Mrs Jamieson went over to the window: 'There he is!' she shouted, pointing down. We ran over to her and there, running down the garden path, lit by the setting sun was young Tom.

We shouted at the top of our voices but he didn't take a blind bit of notice. He was bounding, or loping like, rather than running, and suddenly Mrs Jamieson screamed. 'Look, his shadow, his shadow, it's the shadow of a cat!' Then she fainted at our feet."

Mrs Moore finished up her port and Lemon in one big swig. The rest of us just sat there, looking at our untouched glasses. "Well," I said, "thank you Mrs Moore. Very interesting. Excuse me moment, all." I went upstairs and had a look at the children. Then I put the cat out and locked the back door. Bert wasn't in the sitting room when I got back.

"He's just popped next door to see that Michael's alright." Said Elsie.

We all sat round looking at each other.

"Tell me, Mrs Moore," I said, "Did you ever see Tom again?"

"See him again?" She said.
"Well, I mean, was that shadow..."

"Shadow?! Oh! That wasn't a shadow, that was Thomas. He'd escaped from the vet's and come home all on his own. Dear Thomas."

ONE GOOD RETURN

When I was courting, that's before the war of course, me and Rosy used to spend out weekends getting as far away as we could on my old motor-cycle and combination. Every Sunday we pushed off somewhere. Rosy all tucked up in the cradle and me riding the iron horse, feeling like a knight in armour. As a matter of fact I was a bit fed up when Rosy's dad said she mustn't ride pillion and I had to sell my old sport's job to get the combination, but it wasn't so bad once you got used to the idea.

Well, one Sunday me and Rosy went off to Margate. We had a lovely day. Swimming, tennis, fish and chips, then in the evening we made a few bob at the dogs, and spent them at the Fun Fair on the scenic railway and ice-cream and some more fish and chips. So it was pretty late when we set off for London.

For all that Rosy didn't really start worrying about getting home until we got a puncture, just as we began to leave the Town behind us.

Oh, don't be long, she said, it's getting ever so late, you know how mad dad gets.

All right love, I said, have it fixed in a jiffy. I did an' all. That was the quickest wheel I've ever changed. And we were soon bowling along down the Thanet Way. Singing as we went under the stars, with the warm air full of the scents of the sea and the summer fields. Lovely it was.

Suddenly Rosy screamed - "Look out!" I swerved like a graph at an earthquake and pulled up just beyond the body of a bloke lying half on the road and half on the grass verge.

"Oh," said Rosy, "did you hit him?"

"I don't think so," I said, "I didn't feel a bump did you?"

"No, she said, do you think he's....."

"I don't know," I said, "s'pose I'd better have a look." I got off the bike and walked back a couple of yards to where the feller lay. I didn't need to kneel down by him to know what was wrong. I could smell him from where I stood.

Rosy called after me – "Well, is he.. dead?"

"Yes," I said, "dead drunk."

She joined me by the side of the bloke.

"What shall we do?" she said.

"I don't know," I said, "I suppose we could tuck him up for the night in the ditch."

"Oh we can't do that," says Rosy, "he'd catch his death."

"I doubt it," I said, "he's got enough fuel in him to last Battersea Power Station a week."

"Oh, don't be silly," she said, "you can't just leave a human being lying in the road."

"Oh, all right," I said, "let's see who he is and where he comes from." There wasn't much of anything on him to prove who he was, but by a couple of envelopes in the breast pocket of his jacket we reckoned he must be Mr. E. Pike of 137, Rosecroft Gardens, Tottenham.

"Well," I said to Rosy, "satisfied? Now I suppose we'd better find a police station and hand him in."

"Oh dear". said Rosy.

"Now what's the matter?" I said.

"Nothing – but it's so late all ready – and you know what Dad is."

"Yes, I said, I know. But what d'you want me to do – take him home?"

"Oh aren't you clever thinking of that," she said.

"Eh?" I said.

"What a good idea," she went on, "after all Tottenham's not far from North Finchley is it?"

"I don't know," I said, "it's a big place."

She wasn't listening. "Then we wouldn't have to waste any more time would we, with Police and things like that, I mean."

"Well, I don't know," I said, "you can get into trouble for that sort of thing........"

"And so can he, poor feller," said Rosy. "Come on don't be mean, we can tuck him into the side car and nobody'll be any the worse off. Poor chap, I expect he's just a day tripper, had a few too many at one of those big pubs back on the road and his chara went off without him, so he started walking home."

"Oh all right," I said, "don't make a song and dance about it. Give me a hand and we'll tuck him in the sidecar."

After a few minutes we got on our way again. There wasn't a murmur from Mr. Pike. He was out like a light, sometimes we could hear him snoring a little when the bike was running quiet enough, but all in all it was very pleasant riding through the night with Rosy behind me, her arms around my waist.

Of course it was pretty late by the time I got her home - about half-past one it was. Her Dad was waiting up alright. As a matter of fact he was waiting at the door. I could see his eyes shining like traffic lights stuck at amber as we turned into her road; then when he spotted Rosy on the pillion they turned red. And they were still red when we pulled up at the house.

"Fine time to come home," he said.
"Well," I said, "you see."

"Yes," he said, "I see – I see Rosy on the pillion." Then he must have smelt Mr. Pike "you been drinking?" he said.

"Oh no Dad," said Rosy, "it's Mr. Pike –"

"Mr. who?" he said.

"A gentleman we picked up....."

"Picked up!" said her Dad. "Now look here young man, it's one thing to keep my Rosy out late and another thing to ride her on the pillion, but if you think I'm going to let her mixed up with drunken friends you pick up all over England, you've got another think coming!"

You could hear the door slam from Tally Ho Corner to Barnet Church. I looked at Mr. Pike, snoring his head off now in the sidecar. There was nothing for it; "Come on my 'friend'," I said, "let's get you home."

It took me an hour and a half to find Rosecroft Gardens, Tottenham and it was just gone 3 a.m. when I pulled Mr. Pike out of the side-car and propped him up against the door of number 137. The house was dark and still, so was the whole road for that matter. It was like knocking up a morgue.

After about a quarter of an hour I said to Mr. Pike, well my friend, one more go then I'm off – they can take you in with the milk. And I ripped off a tattoo that would have done 'em proud at Aldershot. Half way through it, lights went on upstairs in the house next door. I stopped as a lady all done up in curlers and clips and a woollen shawl stuck her head out of on of the bright window. "What are you trying to do, she said, wake the dead!?"

"Sorry," I said, "but this is Mr. Pike's house isn't it?"

"That's right," she said, "but it's no use knocking there, he went away with his family, yesterday morning, for a week at Margate."

THE DUMB ANIMAL

Berlin was a strange city in 1939, the time of the "phoney war". I moved in to represent the Steel Corporation; taking over from Eccles who was posted from the London Branch and had to get back there pretty sharpish that August. It wasn't easy to find a billet for me and the family. But in the end I found a little house going in the Tiergarten quarter and hopped in quick with Mary and our small son Harry.

We must have been living there a month or more when Oscar came to stay. We called him Oscar like a film award, you're delighted to get it, but then what the heck can you do with it. Our Oscar was an Alsatian. A great tall dog that must have been living for weeks on his fat and what he could fight the alley dogs for.

His eyes stood out over the bones of his face and his ribs pronged through his coat like the teeth of a plough. He arrived at two o'clock of a Tuesday morning, his claws hit the door like hailstones and the paint and wood were shredded by the time I got out of bed and opened up. And he hardly waited for me to do that, as I turned the lock he shoved the door back and had me hanging from the hat-stand.

We looked at each other for a long moment. Then his lip went up. I moved off the hat-stand and he beat a warning tattoo from the drum skin over his ribs, as he stood there, a cadaver full of growling malevolence.

"Out," I said, holding the door wide. "Go on you hound, get out of here."

Mary came to the top of the stairs as I moved towards him. "What's going on Jimmy?" she said sleepily, and then as Oscar threw back his head and bayed at me, she screamed "no Jimmy don't, don't try to touch him."

"Well what am I supposed to do," I said, "bake a cake?"

She didn't hear me – or didn't want to. "Poor thing," she said, "look he's hardly got anything between bone and skin – and not all that much skin." Quietly she came down to Oscar. He backed away from her grumbling like a subway train you've just missed. Then he stood by the wall and let her hand rest on him as she talked gently. He let het lead him into the kitchen, and I closed the door. Oscar was in.

And those were the terms he stayed on. With Mary there was an armed truce, with me there was a cold war; and Harry we kept out of his way just in case.

One thing soon became very clear, we and Oscar did not speak the same language; whether or not he would have obeyed them, our commands meant nothing to him and our blandishments less. The rattle of dishes and the opening of doors, these things he understood and that was all.

Our friends thought we were crazy and I agreed. Soon nobody would come to the door – I had to bring all the groceries home myself, and go out if I wanted a game of Bridge. Our mail was delivered to the house next door, and Oscar knew a Cop on the beat who'd been very helpful before, but suddenly found a hat-full of regulations we were breaking.

Things got progressively worse until, some months later, it became out turn to move back home. We'd tried every language we could muster on Oscar: French, Italian, German, Czech, even a little Chinese, but he turned really nasty when we tried to sell our interest in the house to a Russian colleague. Out client refused to take the place unless we took Oscar out of it with us.

Back in America, Oscar was, if anything, a little less sociable. Whenever Harry and I went walking, he had to come with us, on a lead, with a muzzle – Mary wouldn't chance his attitude to callers while we were out.

So he was with us on the 4th July when we took a turn around the fair that had come to town. And he nearly had my arm out of its socket diving in and out of the crowd.

He'd never been like this before. Rushing up to all the stalls, and anyone wearing anything like a funny hat – you could see he was looking for someone – not someone to bite, but someone he expected to find here.

Outside a big top a Barker was crying the Show and a bunch of clowns were dishing out a sample of the fun. Suddenly Oscar whimpered and pulled harder. I heaved him to heel. Then he let out a howl of canine agony and struggled like a mad thing on the leash.

Half a dozen people turned and stared, "Brute", said one dear lady "treating a poor dumb animal like.." That was as far as she got. Oscar yanked me off my feet and I cannoned flat into her before he tore away from my grip.

When we sorted ourselves out I found Harry and Oscar up on the platform with the Barker and the clowns. Oscar had his muzzle off and was practically licking lumps off the littlest of the clowns.

"Hey, watch out," I shouted, "he'll eat you."

I got to them and got hold of Oscar's collar. The little clown smiled up at me and Oscar wagged his tail. I'd never seen that happen before. "What goes on here?" I said.

The clown turned to the Barker and his hands and fingers flicked like he was typing it out. The Barker watched him and then told me, "Bo-Bo says that Sacha was his dog in Berlin but got left behind when the Nazis chased him out of Germany for 'Dumb Insolence'."

"Oh yeah," I said, "whereabouts in Berlin?"

Bo Bo played some more tunes on his fingers. "Off the Tiergarten Strasse", said the Barker when he stopped.

"Yes," I said, "that's right – Well tell him we're delighted he's got Sacha back and he's welcome." Bo Bo practically broke his wrists at that one.

"Wait a minute," said the Barker, as he watched – "Bo Bo says he can't keep Sacha now, he's telling him he must be a good dog and go with you and the little boy."

"Well, tell him thanks all the same but." Before I could finish Sacha gave the little clown a big lick, picked up his muzzle and shoved it into my hand, and then went and sat by Harry.

"You've got yourself a dog mister," said the Barker.

Harry looked up at me, so did Sacha, and they were both wagging their tails.

"You must be nutty," I said ".... O.K."

"Yippee," squealed Harry and dived off the platform into the crowd with Sacha on his heels.

"Hey wait a minute," I said to the Barker, "do I have to learn sign language to talk to this animal?"

He turned to the clown – Bo Bo's fingers knitted some more words.

"Bo Bo says that's right," said the Barker..........." in Hungarian!"

THE GAME MUG

Before the war I used to run a pub in the
Midlands. It was a good pub, in a useful spot –
on the way to and from three racecourses. And
of course that's very handy for a pub – there's
always one for luck on the way in and one to
celebrate on the way out – or if there's nothing
to celebrate then 3 or 4 to drown your sorrows.

Well any pub can say that it has some very
funny customers, but I think that was truer
about mine than most. Though I must say I was
surprised when a quiet little geezer who turned
up every day for a beer and a sandwich, racing
or no racing, turned out to be the funniest
customer of the lot.

Civil little chap he was, not a natterer – Good
morning – good day – please, thank you. That
was about all that ever came out of him. Not
that he was stuck up or anything, just what you

might call 'reserved' So it shook me one day, just a little while before the Derby, when he watched me having a go over the form of the runners for a bit, and then said quite suddenly:

"Mug's game."

"Oh?" I said.

"Mug's game racing."

"Oh." I said again, "I didn't think you were interested in the Sport of Kings."

"That's right," he said, "I'm not. Not any more, anyway."

"You used to back horses did you?" I said.

"Worse than that," he answered, "I used to ride 'em."

I think he must have seen I thought he was having me on: "You remember Alec Aston?", he said.
"Well," I said, "you're going back a bit, but I've made a few quid on his mounts in my time – wait a minute there was Kidnapper in the Rubican Plate – I made myself a score or two on that nag half a dozen years ago."
"A dozen," he said.

"A dozen what? I asked.

"A dozen years ago –"

"You sure?" I said.

"I ought to be," he said, "I'm him."

"Well I'm blowed," I said, "I wondered what had happened to you."

"Oh," he said, "things went wrong you know, personal things, nothing to do with racing, but it's a mug's game for all that, and I can prove it.

After a few duff seasons, things weren't coming on any too rosy for the next go on the Flat, so I took myself abroad. A few years back they'd been screaming for me all over the place. But bad news travels fast and practically everywhere I went the only rides anyone remembered were the ones they'd seen me lose. No, the going wasn't anything like easy. I found the best chance I stood of a ride was some place where they'd never heard of me. But then if they hadn't heard of me they didn't want me, so I was on Shanks's Pony going and coming.
Things got worse and worse. Until I reached the obstinate stage – I wasn't going home with my tail between my legs, but if I stayed away much longer there wouldn't be more of me to

come home than you could pack into a saddle bag. I tell you I was practically on the round the dustbin stakes when a Bulgarian ice-cream maker took me on to ride his entry at a dirt track meeting outside Buda-Pest. He must have used the horse on week days on an Okey Pokey round. I didn't see it until I got on the course and by then it was too late, and anyway I was too hungry to change my mind. He was the worst horse in sight, and none of 'em was beautiful.

So, I put a good face on it in the changing room. It was full of jockeys when I went in, all nattering away. Quite a lot of English was being spoken, with various accents, and by then I had enough French and German and Italian to talk my way around. But as I came into the room, that chat sort of petered out. I said Hello, but apart from a couple of Guten Tags, a buon' giorno and a 'Hiyah' nobody said anything at all.

As I changed, the conversation picked up again but in mutters – and if I caught anybody's eye he'd stop even muttering. There was one busy bloke who was going around having a word with everybody in turn, and now and then I'd catch something like – O.K. I'll take 10, then 25 for me, Jimmy – or yeah I'll have fifty. Of course I knew what the game was. I'd done it myself in those last years: they were carving up the race.

Now get this straight, I didn't mind them fixing a crooked race but what really got me griping was that they weren't cutting me in on it. Nobody came near me. In the weighing-in room, in the paddock, in the parade, they treated me like a poor relation at a wedding. By the time we got to the starting post, I was red with rage. I was going to show these mottled cowboys how a top British jockey should be treated. Even if he was on a bag of bones and hadn't been a top anything for quite a long time.

At the off I was ready to ride my poor nag three times round the Aintree course with an extra Beechers Brook for luck. After a couple of furlongs, I wasn't so sure. At three furlongs he was puffing like a leaking foot-pump and his ribs were working like the bellows of a concertina. By the fourth furlong I was making excuses to myself and dropping back.

But at the fifth I was still in the race. My old mount was practically out on his feet, but the others weren't much better off. I took him round the outside and made a run. The jockey on a big grey that was rolling like an old tanker heard me coming and crossed me. I nearly went over my horse's neck reining in, but before he could recover I made a dash for the space he'd left inside him and I got through, but as I went by he aimed a cut with his whip at my horse's neck. I reached forward and took it across my knuckles.

It hurt like the devil but I didn't care, I was through the first line. Ahead of me were the leaders. I made for a space between two of them but they closed me out. I went for the rails but the jockey lying first bore over and my left foot hit the wood and I nearly lost my stirrup.

Well it was blood now. I was going to break through if it killed me, or my horse – or any one of them that fouled me up again. I was just gathering my poor brute together for a last smash through when a foot of daylight opened out in from of me, and then it was a yard. They must be crazy. I roared through it laughing at them and I took the race by a length and a half.

I was still laughing back in the changing room. 'Well,' I said, as I chucked my gear on the floor, 'that'll teach you not to cut a buddy out on the carve up, just because he's a stranger in these parts. Quite apart from trying to kill me on the course.' "

"Just tactics my friend," said one of the local boys – "we all had our money on you to win!"

NETE
CONFUNDIT
ILLIGIMITII

THE OLD SCHOOL TIE

I haven't always been my own boss, or anybody's boss at all for that matter. But I've worked hard and straight for most of my life – when I was a kid we left school at 13, but I was doing odd jobs round the East End of London long before then.

So now, when things are coming a bit easier, I feel I've earned it. And although I don't live in the East End any more, I often wish that I'd been able to pick up the education to appreciate the more gracious things of life while I was earning them.

So one thing I determined very early on in my married life. Whatever I was missing my kids wouldn't. They'd have all the chances I didn't get. As it turned out we only had the one, our boy, Michael. And like I promised myself, when the time came he went to a public school.

It was a good public school and it did him a lot of good (of course his mother and me were no better than most parents of an only child) but term after term you could see him steadily getting less of a spoilt brat and more of a young man who could live with his fellow men on their own terms, without losing his own personality or becoming just one of a mob.

There was one boy at the school, been there a couple of terms before Michael arrived, who he chummed up with right away. His name was Drover and Mike's letters were full of him – Drover this and Drover that. And they stayed pals all through their school-days.

At home during the holidays Mike used to tell us more about his friend. It seemed that he lived in a big house in the country. A Manor house it was and his father was sort of squire of the village and the farms all around it. So when Mike wrote from school one term that he'd been invited to spend the Easter holidays at Drover's place we could hardly refuse, although we were a bit sad at not having him at home.

We missed him more somehow during the holiday time than when he was away at school. I suppose we'd come to look forward to his holidays so much. But you can imagine how pleased we were to get a letter from Mr Drover inviting us to go and stay with him for the last week-end of the holidays before Mike was due back at school – he had to come home for all his summer kit before the new term began, and we could take him back with us.

Well, we really looked forward to it. In fact, I think my wife got over-excited about the idea. Anyway by the Thursday before we were due to go she'd worked herself up to a fine high temperature. The doctor called it 'flu, but I still say it was psychological. Of course, I said I wouldn't go. Mike could very well come home by himself. To tell you the truth I was a bit nervous about going alone – I've never been very good at butlers and footmen and all that sort of thing – even to this day I always take a quick look at the wife before I tackle a meal laid up for more than four courses. But she wouldn't hear of me not going. "You go," she said, "go and enjoy yourself."

Enjoy myself! Still, in the end I went. And d'you know, I was jolly glad I did, right from the moment I got there. They picked me up at the station in an old Rolls Royce. Mr. Drover was with the boys, and I shared the back seat with a cocker spaniel. There was no question of anything starchy or stuck-up. I hadn't enjoyed a weekend like it for years. Mr. Drover showed me all over his estate and we talked about crops and cows, and politics and cigars, everything you could lay tongue to. I scarcely saw Mike, but I knew he was having a good time and I could see why.

I was sorry when the time came for us to bundle and go. And as Drover and I were having our last chat on the Monday morning, I spoke to him of something that had been on my mind since he met me at the station. "Mr. Drover," I said, "I haven't liked to say this before, because people often say it when they're trying to pry into other people's affairs and I shouldn't like you to think that such was my intention."

"My dear Jackson," he said, "by all means say whatever you like."

"Well Mr. Drover," I said, "ever since we met, I've had a feeling that this isn't the first time. Of course I'm in a fair way of business and maybe it was at a Board Meeting – or on some Charity Committee."
"My dear Jackson," he said, "of course we've met before, and we knew each other very well – but when we were at the Mile End Road Council School together, your name wasn't Jackson – nor mine Drover. But you might say we have the same Old School Tie"

THE OTHER CHEEK

Have you ever been left with the lot to do on a Monday. The washing, the beds, the lunch, the pots, the pans, the lot? Well I hadn't until one weekend last summer. The phone went on the Sunday night and it's the Mrs' brother-in-law, saying will she go over and help her sister settle in with the new baby when she comes home from the hospital on Monday morning.

Well, of course, no woman can resist that and so I'm left, at crack of dawn, with Angela to get off to school and young Michael to keep amused for the rest of the day. "And remember" says the wife, "if he gets on your nerves, don't lose your temper with him."

"Temper," I said, "what temper?"

"Yes," she said, "I know all about that, but temper or no temper – don't you lose it."

Now I've always thought that the Mrs. Laid it on a bit thick about young Mike, proper little devil she made him out to be, but all I could say was that he looked like an Angel when I used to get home at night and see him asleep in bed, and I used to look forward to him climbing in with me in the morning to have a fairy tale read to him, before I had to get off to work.

So that Monday morning it was all good fun for me getting him dressed and turning his empty egg-shell upside down at breakfast and playing "look you haven't started". The first little wisp of cloud across the sun came when I started up the washing machine and there was a squall from the cat as the revolving arms at the bottom of the thing plucked her off the ground by her tail and swung her around like a banjo with fur on and making roughly the same sort of noise. What was she doing in there? "Stupid cat," I said to Mike after I'd stopped the machine.

"She was drinking her milk," he said.

"Silly of me to put it there," I said. Then I remembered that I hadn't put it there. I looked at Michael – but I couldn't prove anything. All the same I pushed him off into the kitchen and left him with some flour and stuff to make some pastry. Michael was great on pastry;

whenever I grumbled at having to eat the grubby jam tarts he'd made, the wife said "don't moan it's the only way I can keep Michael quiet while I'm working."

So I thought I'd try it – didn't work this time though.

I finished the washing and went back into the kitchen. There he was papering the walls with a mixture of flour and water and the daily paper. I proper read the riot act to him then, and he was very subdued as he came out to help me hang up the washing.

If course I couldn't be sure that he knocked the foot of the clothes prop away on purpose, but the prop end hit me flat on the head and as I sat in the yard looking at all the wet laundry around me dragging in the dirt, I felt it was all too much of a coincidence, particularly when I caught sight of the grin on his face, That was the last straw.

Temper or no temper, I picked up a wet shirt. He took one look at me and scooted. I went chasing after him into the scullery. His little blue pants were just disappearing into the kitchen as I got there and I took a swipe at them with the wet shirt. I didn't get him, but he must have known I meant it by the slap of the shirt on the shelf over the kitchen door which was where it stuck. Anyway he came back through the kitchen door snivelling a bit and mumbling "I'm sorry Daddy, I didn't mean it … I'm sorry Daddy". Don't you talk to me, I said, I'll tan your hide, I pulled the shirt free from the shelf and all the pots and pans that were up there, came down with it.

The whole shoot landed square on top of Michael, and he sat down on the kitchen floor with a howl. And to make matters worse a vegetable grater tangled in the tail of the shirt and as I jerked it clear, it scratched along the side of his face and ploughed little red furrows down his cheek.

All my temper went like the last fizzle of a soda siphon, all I could think of now was the poor little kid, and what his mum would say.

And I'd just about got Michael and the placed tidied up a bit when in she came. Michael, she said, what's happened to your face – he lowered his eyes looking at me from under his curling lashes. Then: "I fell over in the garden", he said.

NEVER GIVE A SUCKER...

It's a long, long time since I tried journalism as a career. In fact this story happened so long ago that I would probably have forgotten it by now, if it wasn't for the tragedy.

It all started on one of those glorious spring days that make a young man feel good. Indeed, I was feeling so good that even when Knocker - he was the only reporter on the paper junior to me - told me that Mac wanted to see me, I didn't get that 'doomed' feeling that usually accompanied a summons to the editor's office. And when I knocked at Mac's door his usual 'Enterrr', sounded almost jovial.

"Ah, Slaterrr," he said, I think I've got a job rrright up yourrr street.

I made the usual noises.

"Yes," he said. "I'm told yourrr a bit of a gambler."

For a horrible moment I thought he was referring to some of the entries on my expense account. "Look Mac," I said, "I had to take that Taxi to Euston and I didn't have time to get a receipt. I ...."

"I'm not talking about your expense account," Mac said. "Not at the moment anyhow. No, I've chosen you to investigate the tale that Knocker brought in, about that gambling establishment in Mayfair."

"But Mac," I said, "That costs ..."

"You know the angle," he went on, "servicemen with a bit of pay in their pockets, innocent young females looking for excitement, with their allowance burning a hole in their purses..."

"But Mac," I tried again "I don't ...."

"The lure of the lights, the click of the ball in the wheel, the bated hush of expectancy...."

"Mac," I said "why don't you write it, then nobody need bother to go..."

Mac looked at me hard. "Sometimes," he said, "in newspapermen, cynicism is mistaken for wit.

This is a fundamentally vicious business; the root of more crime and vice than any other source, except drugs, and to some it's just as addictive."

"I'm sorry Mac, "I said, I'm not trying to be funny but look I'm overdrawn already and...."

"I'll arrange for you to draw five ...£250. from accounts."

"That's great," I said.

"And this time, sign your own name!"

I went.

Back in the newsroom, Knocker was narking, and I couldn't blame him really. "Well, I reckon it's not fair! After all, I'm the one that got the lead. £250. Blimey! Fanny and I could have had...."

"That's probably why Mac is sending me and not you," I said, "come on, give me the details."

Knocker described it all to me and finished up with "And when you get there, you knock three times and ask for Lucy."

"Knock three times and ask for Lucy?" I said.

"Yeah. Does sound a bit old fashioned doesn't it? But that's what I was told."

I did wonder whether or not I was being set up for something, but I followed directions and it all worked. The door opened right on cue. On the other side of it was a big bruiser with two cauliflower ears and a nose that looked like something very heavy had sat on it!

"Well?" he said.

"Not really," I replied, "I've got a bit of a cold! What do you mean 'Well?' I was told to knock three times and ask for Lucy."

"That's me," he said. And when he saw the expression on my face he smiled; "It's short for Lucien. I can't help it if my mother was fanciful, can I? Want to play?"

"That's right," I said, and brought out ten of the twenty-five nice new tenners I'd got from the accounts department.

"We'll soon change those for you," Lucien said, and took me to an office where they changed my £100 for a bowl full of tiddley winks; each colour being worth a different amount - from £1. to £20.

So off I went with my chips and to tell you the truth, I had one of the best nights out I've had in years. I played at all the tables, I had plenty to eat, plenty to drink, the company was quiet but amusing, the service was as smooth as a well oiled ball-bearing, and after about four hours, when I cashed in my chips, I was on the receiving end of *fifteen* ten pound notes, and I'd only given them ten to begin with. Of course, they weren't nice new ones like I'd handed in, but they still came to £150 when you added them up.

It may have been the small hours of the morning, and it may have been only Spring, but it was calm, clear and crisp and I was feeling good. The streets were well lit and I set off for home down St. James' and the embankment. As I walked I began to get a bit worried. What was I going to say to Mac? I'd been sent out to get an exposé and all I had to show was a blooming good evening and £50. profit. I knew old Mac, he'd swear I'd done it on purpose.

I was just beginning to feel depressed over the whole business when I noticed a girl in front of me leaning over the Embankment rail. At least, that was what I thought when I first noticed her. By the time I'd taken a few more paces I realised that she was climbing over it.

Well, this was too good a night to have spoilt by that sort of catastrophe. Tomorrow would be bad enough, with Mac to deal with; so I made a dive for her. She didn't struggle or make a sound. I remember thinking that in her own mind she was already twenty-feet down, in the silent, black waters of the River Thames.

I half carried her back to a seat, a shadowed one, half way between two lamps and not really lit by either, and we sat there while I babbled heaven knows what nonsense and rubbed her cold hands.

I heard heavy, even footsteps approaching and caught the reflection of a light on a policeman's helmet. There was only one thing to do. I took her in my arms and cradled her head in the bend of my arm, so that she couldn't move, and then I kissed her. I stayed kissing her until the footsteps had gone past us. That was the first time she'd struggled since I pulled her back from the brink.

"What the Hell do you think you're doing?" She spat at me.

"Saving you from a lot of awkward questions from the local Bill" I said. "I reckon if there's any questions to be asked I'll ask them. What were you doing back there? There's no safety net you know. It's just cold and wet."

"Why did you stop me?" she said.

"Lady" I replied, "I've just had a wonderful evening. I've eaten well, drunk well, gambled and won. It's not very often that all these things happen to me at once, and when they do, suicide, even if not my own, is *not* a fitting conclusion."

She looked at me for a moment; almost a calculating look. I saw all the wisdom and sorrow of womanhood in her face, and then she began to tell me her story. It was the usual tale of hope and disillusion; of dreams being shattered by reality; of broken relationships and a broken heart. I'd heard it all before; believe me you don't have to work on a newspaper to hear it either. Stories like this never even make the afternoon editions. But there was something about this girl: maybe it was the drink, maybe it was pity, maybe it was the kiss ...Whatever, I decided that I needed time to think about it and daylight to see it in.

A taxi came cruising up towards us. I whistled it and as it stopped peeled off three of the £10 notes - that still left £20. profit, so Mac couldn't grumble. I put them in her hand, made her repeat the office 'phone number until she knew it and directed the taxi to take her to a cheap hotel where she'd still be able to get in.

So next morning I got to the office early, just in case she was an early riser. I knew already what the girl meant to me, I suppose I'd known the night before, but this was more sober judgement. By nine o'clock I was already beginning to worry. Knocker arrived. "Hello old boy, what's the matter, couldn't you sleep, or was the story too hot to keep? 250 quid. You might have cut me in you know."

"I'll cut your throat if you don't shut up" I snapped.

"Oh all right. I was only...."

"Well don't," I said, as Jimmy the tea boy dashed in.

"Mac wants you right away, Johnny," he said.

I clipped him over the ear as I got up. "Mr Mac to you" I said, and headed for the office.

"Well," Mac said, "What did you get?"

"Nothing" I said. "Do you mind if I use your 'phone?" and I picked it up before he had time to object. "It's Johnny," I said to the girl on the switchboard, "if a young lady 'phones and asks for me, I'm in Mr MacLoch's office."

"Nothing eh?" said Mac. "And how much did this 'nothing' cost the paper?"

"Another nothing", I replied. "I actually made a profit of fiff... er twenty quid. The place is on the level Mac. So all right, they gamble. If you want to expose that, go ahead, but if you're looking for a den of vice and loaded dice, you'll have to look somewhere else."

"You'll be recommending I go there for a good evening's entertainment next." Said Mac.

"You could do a lot worse," I replied, "I tell you, they play to the rules.

"That lot only ever play to one rule - 'never give a sucker an even break'."

"All right," I said, "What does that make me?"

"It makes you a fool," he said, "a fool who can't see beyond the glass in his hand or deeper than the slots in a roulette wheel."

"Lay off me Mac," I said. "I've got things on my mind."

"Cobwebs," he replied. "They always accumulate in disused corners. Well, get out and see if you can get any 'things' onto paper."

Back at my desk I couldn't wait any longer. I 'phoned the hotel: "My name's Slater," I said, "a young lady came in at about 2 o'clock this morning. I'd like to speak to her please."

"Name please?"

"Slater,"

"The young lady's name." Said the voice

I paused. "I'm sorry, I don't know it."

"Surprise, surprise."

"Look, I said," you don't get many customers at 2 o'clock in the morning..."

"Certainly not nameless young ladies."

"Please," I said, "will you help? It means a lot to me."

The voice suddenly got human; "I'm sorry sir," it said, "but we have had no registrations since 10.45 last night."

"Thanks." I said, and put down the receiver. I'd expected it somehow. All through the night a kind of aching worry had been growing - I'd hoped it was only a hangover. But now I began to feel mad. Mad at her for letting me down and mad at myself for being taken for such an easy ride. Maybe Mac was right: 'Never give a sucker an easy break' and I was the sucker. Yet she didn't seem that kind. It couldn't have all been an act. Why should it have been?

For a while I sat my desk doing nothing, except making typing noises whenever anyone looked like interrupting me. You see, I didn't know where I'd been hit: if it was my vanity, well I deserved all that I got. But if it wasn't; if it wasn't.....

By about 11 o'clock, just after Jimmy had slopped in with the morning tea, I knew that I couldn't leave it just like that. I had to know. I had to be sure. First of all I rang round the City and West End cab ranks and left messages that I wanted to speak to the cabby who'd picked up a fare on the Embankment at about 2 a.m. and had been asked to take her to Wendell's Hotel. Then I checked the hospitals and the police stations. St George's Hospital had had one female in during the night: she had been celebrating her 72nd birthday and had cut her hand on a glass, in the Elephant and Castle. The police had nothing.

Then, last of all, I rang Denison. A pal of mine on the Mortuary Records. "Anything in last night, Denny?" I said.

"Why, have you lost something?"

"No, nothing special, just trying to appease a hungry editor."

"Hold on Johnny," he said. I could hear the sound of pages turning and Denny humming 'Don't Cry for me Argentina'. Then: "Yes, Here's one: Female, dark, about twenty-two, body recovered from the Thames at 7 a.m. after about four hours immersion." My blood ran as cold as the spring Thames water. "That's all I can offer you Johnny boy," he went on, "Isn't that a dainty dish to set before an editor?"

I didn't answer. It needn't be her of course. It needn't be her.
"Hey, Johnny, you still there?" The 'phone squawked in my ear.

"Yeah, I'm with you Denny. Any identification?"

"No, not even a designer label."

"Peculiarities?"

"If she had any, she took 'em with her. Oh, hang on, she had three tenners stuffed in her bra."

"Three tenners?"

"Yes. Now I'd call that fair to middling peculiar."

"But why would anyone jump in the river if they've got thirty quid to keep them going?"

"That's what I mean," he said. "Ah, it appears..." I could hear him reading to himself: "Yes, they were all duds."

"Duds?!"

"Yeah, you know, forgeries."

Denny went on talking but I put the receiver down. Forgeries. I took the roll of tenners from my pocket and as I looked carefully at each one, my stomach curled up into a small, tight ball of fear. Suddenly I realised that someone was standing at my desk. I looked up. It was a taxi driver.

"You wanted to speak to me guv'nor," he said.

"Wanted to ... Oh, no, it's alright."

"I don't get it," he said, "The office said ... hang on, *I* want a word with *you*. I reckon you owe me five quid. That's two quid for coming here and three quid for that fare last night, I don't change dud tenners, and that was all she had." He looked at the pile of £10. notes on my desk. "They all dud as well?" he asked.

"Yes," I said, "Every last one of them."

Mac reckoned it was the best piece I ever wrote for the paper. It was also the last. I quit the next day!

SUMMER MIST

"Ghosts!" I used to say, "The hysterical reaction of a hyperactive mind to unexpected stimuli." I used to ....

It started last summer - or to be exact the Summer before, when I got terribly sunburnt and as a result missed out on a budding holiday romance. So last Summer I broke the habit of a lifetime, and instead of going for sun, sand and sangria I opted for the fresh air of the Austrian Tyrol. A walking holiday. And if the girls in hiking shorts and sensible boots didn't have quite the same glow as those in bikinis, well, it had still been a wonderful holiday; and somehow I felt that there was a greater sincerity in the relationships I'd formed.

But now it was nearly over. A few days more and it would be packing-up time. I felt wonderful. I'd eaten well, drunk less than usual on holiday, and walked up and down more hills and valleys than I'd ever seen before. I was fitter than I had been for years; and I had a number to 'phone when I got home that looked like being much more than just a holiday romance. And if the evenings seemed to be a bit mistier than at the start of the holiday, so what? In my world, it was definitely sunny.

Two days before I was due to leave I decided to tackle the small but steep mountain at the back of the hotel. It wasn't a climb, just a very steep walk and the map showed a path all the way to the top. It should take about four hours each way, so if I left at about seven in the morning I should be back in time for tea, even allowing an hour for lunch.

That evening I asked Walter - who wouldn't answer unless you pronounced it 'Valter' - for a picnic for the next day.

"Where are you going?" he asked.

"Just out the back," I said. "I've been saving that mountain for the end."

He frowned a little. "You will need to leave early," he said, "the mists are beginning to come down early now."

"Don't worry," I said. "I'll have breakfast at six, leave by seven and be back for tea."

"Good," he said. "Our mountain looks beautiful in the sunlight. It's not so friendly in the dark."

That night I left my rucksack at the reception desk, and collected it again as I left the next morning. As usual it was well packed, so that nothing would roll around as I walked, and I knew that it contained a selection of fresh foods that would be nourishing and sustaining, without making me feel too full. Packed lunches for hill walkers were one of the hotel's specialities; and they were very good at it.

As I left, the manager greeted me. "I hear you're going up our mountain," he said. "You will be careful, won't you. The mists are coming down earlier now."

"Don't worry," I said. "I'll be back for tea." And off I strode, without a care in the world.

As I reached the foothills I passed an old shepherd, harvesting the rich summer grasses to feed his sheep through the winter. "You're going up the mountain?" He said. "Be careful....."

"I know," I laughed. "The mists are coming down earlier now. I've promised to be back in time for tea." And on I went. Somehow, I was conscious of his eyes following me as I went. Just one more thing that didn't bother me.

It was a perfect day for walking. The sky was clear blue, but the sun wasn't too hot. The breeze was refreshing, but never chilled. Butterflies hovered and swooped, birds sang and crickets chirruped. I didn't know whether God was in his Heaven, but certainly all was well with the world.

By half-past ten I was nearing the summit. The path I was following suddenly widened out into a flat clearing, where a couple of other paths also seemed to arrive. There were some flat rocks there and I decided that on the way down this would be where I stopped for lunch.

In half an hour I was at the top and taking the mandatory photos of the panorama below me. And so back down to my dining room, warmed by the sun, with music by the massed bands of birds and insects. I laid out my lunch: fruit juice; a selection of cold meats with salads to accompany; some cheeses and a small piece of cake, which I knew would melt in the mouth. There was a quarter bottle of local red wine and a slightly larger bottle of sparkling water. A feast fit for a king! I wined and dined and sat back, feeling very contented, to count my blessings.

Somewhere along the way, I must have got side-tracked into counting sheep, for I woke with a start, feeling cold and wondering who'd turned the lights out. I realised that I had committed a cardinal sin, and gone to sleep on the mountain. Nobody had turned the lights out; there were millions of them right above me; they were called stars and they were hidden from me, as was everything else, by the mist.

I thought I'd met Fear before, as I hurtled down roller coasters, or scuba dived into dark caves, but I'd never met anything like this fear. It screwed my stomach into a tight knot, shoved my heart into my mouth and totally altered my breathing pattern.

"Now hang on." I said to myself. "You're up a mountain. All you have to do is follow the path that goes *down* and you'll be all right. Simple."

I gathered up the debris of my lunch, found the rock face and followed it round until it stopped.

"Here we are," I said. "Path." Off I set. I'm not old enough to remember those 'pea-souper' smogs we used to get; but they couldn't have been thicker than this. 'Mist' was a total misnomer. Whether it was cloud or fog I didn't know. What I did know, however, was that it was dense. I couldn't even see my feet, let alone the stones that kept tripping me up before rolling away, laughing, down the hill. But it was one of those stones that saved my life: it was bigger and firmer than the others that had made me stumble; this one tripped me up completely. I measured my length on the hard mountain path and was very conscious of the hard ground beneath me. Then I became even more conscious of the fact that there wasn't any hard ground beneath my outstretched arms. The ground stopped somewhere around my elbows. My hands were just waving in space. Slowly I withdrew them from their nothing and felt around. I was sitting about a foot from the edge of what seemed to be a precipice. If I'd met Fear at my lunch-stop, I was now meeting his big brother. I didn't know what to do or which way to turn. I hadn't passed any precipices on the way up; so where had this one come from? And then I remembered - those two other paths that converged at that clearing: I'd taken one of the wrong paths!

There was only one thing for it; I had to retrace my steps. The only trouble was that that fall had so shaken me, I didn't really know where I'd come from. For all I knew, precipices surrounded me. There was only one option: I started to crawl.

In ten minutes my hands and knees were bleeding; my back was aching and I was convinced that I was going to die on that mountain.

I don't know whether I had actually started praying, but suddenly, like the answer to a prayer, a shepherd boy appeared through the mist. He didn't speak; he just smiled, beckoned and turned back the way he had come. Scrambling to my feet, I followed.

He must have known that mountain like the back of his hand - if not better. He found his way through that infernal fog like it didn't exist; and while I stumbled and slipped he seemed almost to float over the rocks, so sure were his feet. He set a pace I'd have found difficult to keep up with in broad daylight. But Fear was at my shoulder, goading me on. To lose sight of him was to lose everything, so I kept him in sight, no matter what the cost in pain. The path went ever downward and suddenly I realised that we were no longer on hard stones but on grass; we had reached the meadows that lay like a green skirt around the mountain's lower limbs.

The boy stopped, suddenly, and I saw light streaming from an open door just ahead. In it I saw my saviour for the first time: He was about twenty years old, wearing typical shepherd's garb of cord trousers and a sheepskin jacket. His feet were bare. His hair was blonde and down to his shoulders, and as he turned the light reflected in his eyes; they were the greenest eyes I had ever seen on a human. Like a cat's eyes. And suddenly he was gone. Back into the fog. Before I even had a chance to stammer out my exhausted thanks.

I turned and staggered towards the open doorway. As I stumbled up the steps the old shepherd whom I had seen that morning, came and helped me in. His wife brought me a hot drink and slowly I came back to life.

"I'm sorry to trouble you," I said. I was very silly and got lost on the mountain. Your door was open and..."

"Our door is always open," said the shepherd. "For ten years it has never shut. Ever since our son was lost on the mountain. On a night just like this." He nodded towards the fireplace and on the shelf above it was an old photograph of a typical shepherd boy; wearing a sheepskin jacket and cord trousers. Even though the photo' was black and white it was clear that the boy had blonde hair, which came down to his shoulders.

"How old was he?" I asked.

"In the picture, eleven." said his father. Today would be his birthday. He would have been twenty-one."

"Tell me," I said, "What colour were his eyes?"

"Ah," said his mother, "his eyes were most unusual. They were green, just like a cat's......"

"Ghosts!" I always say, "Of course I believe in them. Don't you?"

THE SPOTTED DOG

Bank holidays don't always turn out the way you want them to, do they? I mean, we've all sat for hours, pickling in exhaust fumes on a motorway that feels more like a car park, under a sun that's demonstrating global warming; or had a lovely picnic listening to the rain tap-dancing on the leaves of the big Oak tree we're sheltering under. To say nothing of "Oh Alf, the mayonnaise has leaked all over the fruit cake!"

But on the other hand, look what happened to old Frank, last year: Him and his missus and me and my other-half had been away together for every Bank Holiday since I took chalks at the local pub and got Frank as a partner in the next four of darts.

But last year I had some extra holiday due to me, so Ethel and I decided to make a week of it: Bank Holiday Monday to the following

Sunday - and Frank and Jennie decided that, rather than break up the party half-way through the day, because we were the ones with a car, they wouldn't go away at all. To tell you the truth they were a bit peevy about it, but it was the first week away that Ethel and I had had for some time, and we were looking forward to it.

So I didn't see Frank again until a couple of Sundays later, when I called in for him on my way up to the pub for one before lunch. "He's up in the bedroom," said Jennie. In the bedroom?

I went upstairs and found him in bed, looking miserable. He had a bandage over one hand and two long strips of plaster on each cheek.

"What happened to you?" I asked.

"Bank Holiday!" He replied.

"What did you do?" I said, "I thought you were going to have a nice quiet time."

"All I did was go for a walk" he said. "Just went for a walk ....

"I left home," said Frank, "about ten, and headed up towards the fields. There wasn't a soul anywhere. Everything was as quiet and empty as the inside of a politician's head. Then, as I was coming to the end of those new houses they've been building up the hill, I heard the sound of a kid crying. It was a lonely little noise, when everything else was so quiet. Break your heart it would. So I went up to the door of the last house and standing there the noise sounded quite loud.

'Now mind your own business Frankie,' I said to myself; 'half the trouble in the world is caused by people poking their noses into other people's business.' But then I thought, 'and the other half is caused by people looking on and saying it's no concern of mine.'

Then I saw a low front window pushed out a bit on its hinge - you know, the sideways opening kind. So I went over to it, lifted the bar and opened it a bit wider. I could see right across a fair-sized lounge hall, into a big room with parquet flooring. A boy about eight years old was sitting on a beanbag, crying his eyes out. I called out to him - 'Hey!'

He came over, sniffing in Morse code and wiping his soggy sleeve over his eyes and nose.
'What are you crying for?' I said. 'Big boys like you don't cry. Don't be a missy.'

'I'm not crying,' he said as he polished his nose a bit more with his sleeve.

'Where's your mum and dad?' I asked, and that started him hollerin' all over again. 'Here, here,' I said. 'Don't carry on like that; open the door and we'll talk about it.'

'Can't open the door,' he blubbered. 'Dad's put a safety lock on it.'

'Well what's the window left open for?' I said.

'Mum always leaves it open a bit, in case dad forgets the key.'

'Oh, I see,' I said. 'Well, I suppose I'd better come in the window.'

He opened it a bit wider, and in I climbed. It was a nice house. Friendly and well furnished. We went into the parquet-floored room, which I reckon was the lounge. It had a sofa, a couple of easy chairs and a big French window which was wide open! 'Now,' I said, 'come on. What's the trouble?'

'Well, you see,' he said, 'Mum arranged for me to go over to Aunty Edith's and play with my cousin Mark, as they're not going away, so this morning, after Mum, Dad and my brother and sister had all gone off in the car, I went to Aunty's on my bike.'

'So what are you doing here then?' I said.

'Well, when I got there the doctor was just leaving and Aunty sent me straight back because Mark's got the measles.'

I was about to say something, but before the words came out the biggest spotted dog in the world came bouncing in through the French windows. Full of fun he was, 'till he spotted me; then all seven stone of him landed on my chest and down I went, flat on my back. The Indian rug thing on which I landed softened my fall, but you don't really bother how hard a floor is when you've got two paws like canoe paddles with claws in, balanced neatly on either side of your nose, and the largest number of the longest teeth you've ever seen, crunching up and down, just in front of your nose, like a pair of portcullises in the Bloody Tower!

'Don't worry about him', said the boy. 'He's all right.'

'Oh I'm not worried about him,' I said, sweating profusely. 'Grrrr.' went the dog. 'The only trouble is', the boy went on, 'he won't let you up.'

'Don't be daft,' I said. 'Call him off.'

He did. 'Kong, Kong, Kong.' He called, and the animal ambled off me.

'*King* Kong, I suppose,' I said.

'That's right.' Said the boy.

I sat up. And immediately had a chest full of Kong again.

'See what I mean?' said the boy. 'Grrrr.' Said the dog.

I saw what both of them meant. Then suddenly the kid got the giggles. Well, it was nice to see a smile on his face for a change, but I rather wished he'd found something else to laugh at.

'Look,' I said, 'don't just sit there laughing, go and find someone who can get this animal off me.

'Who?' He asked.

'I don't care,' I said, 'I'll even settle for a copper.'

'All right,' he said, and off he went, out of the hall window. Halfway through it he stuck two

- 102 -

fingers in his mouth and let rip with a whistle that would have stopped half the taxis in Oxford Street. 'Charley!' he shouted, 'where are you going?' I heard the answer very faintly: 'Down to the fields coming?'

'Hold on, I'll get my bike.'

'Hey!' I hollered, 'what about me? Go and get that policeman.' But he was gone. There was nothing left but prayer - and the spotted dog. He was sitting roughly on my stomach now, with his paws on my shoulders. 'There's an oozum, woozum, poosam Kong,' I said. 'There's a lovely basket of sugar and spice.' He dribbled on me! 'There's a lovely great chotcham, smotcham boy,' I said, taking it like a man.

He yawned. Then he got an itch. Have you ever had a dog sitting on your stomach, scratching itself? Well, I'm ticklish anyway, and as he got his right, back leg somewhere up around his right ear, his left back leg was beating time in my ribs. So there was me, laughing and wriggling and him scratching and growling. I don't know how much of that I could have stood, but as I put my hands across my waistcoat - you know, that brown fancy one I wear on Saturdays - to try and keep him away from the ticklish spots, I suddenly felt something hard and square in one of the pockets. It was a piece of that fruit and nut that we had at the spurs match about a month ago. So I dug it out and gave Kong a bit. He ate it. For a minute I loved him - he could have had my next month's sweet ration. I threw another little bit a couple of feet away from me and he went for it. I sat up. He landed with all four feet on my shoulders and I lay down again, but I didn't mind - so long as I had a bit of chocolate left I knew how I could move him.

At that moment I heard feet that sounded as if they were walking with their toes clenched. I screwed my head round and there, coming across the hall, like a pair of pantomime villains, were a couple of blokes who looked like punch-bags with knobs on. They didn't spot me at first. Then they saw Kong and stopped dead, like kids playing statues. 'Huff, Huff, Huff,' went Kong. 'Lovely men; sorry I can't come and say hello, but I've got to watch this son of a whatsit here.' That's what he meant, but they didn't get it. 'What you doing 'ere?' the one with the cauliflower said.

'What are *you* doing here's more like it?' I said. We're 'ere legitimate,' was the reply.

'Well on that basis,' I said, 'I don't mind admitting I'm an accident.'

'You mean you're ripping the wrong garment.

'I'm what?'

'Doing the wrong job. Cracking the wrong crib.'

'Look,' I said, 'I don't rip garments, I don't crack cribs and the only job I do lasts me forty hours a week, forty-eight weeks a year. All I want to do is get out from under this dog. 'Grrr.' Said Kong.

'Good little - I mean big doggie,' said the cauliflower.

'Huff, huff, huff,' said my nightmare.

Well, they did the joint. Upstairs, downstairs. Television, stereo system, half a bottle of scotch and three of gin, with mixers; bits of silver from the kitchen, the pop-up toaster and matching coffee percolator. The lot. They stripped the place. They even took the rug and left me on the parquet floor. And Kong just sat on my stomach, smiling at everybody except me, like a duke at a prize-giving. They took the safety lock off the front door, loaded the stuff into a van, put the lock back, slammed the door behind them and went. The house looked like a garden after a March storm!

I heard the van pulling away, and then I started work. There was only one square of chocolate left. I broke off a corner with my thumb nail and flipped it towards the French Window. He went for it, but it was so small I reckon he hardly knew he'd had it - and he was back so quickly that I hardly knew he'd gone! That left me with enough for two more tries at the window. I needed them. The first one hit the curtain and dropped back into the room, but the second was a bullseye; straight out into the garden it sailed leaving me with double top - and did I double! I got that lounge door shut and locked before he'd had time to sort the nuts from the fruit and was backing out of the hall window like a rocket, when suddenly I heard the voice.

'What do you think you're up to?'

I turned round; it was a policeman. 'Constable' I said, 'constable, did you see those men driving a van away from here? they've been burgling the house.'

'Oh yes,' he said. 'And what were you doing, the housework?'

'No, I went in because I heard this kid crying....' then I caught sight of the boy - 'he'll tell you,' I said.

'Me, crying?' said the kid. 'Big boys don't cry. I'm not a sissy.'

At that moment I realised which half of the world is right! 'Look, I said, I got in there to help the kid and the dog's been sitting on me ever since.'

'Are you sure your pals hadn't doped him?' sneered the policeman

'Oh Kong!' shouted the kid, rushing in through the window, 'Kong, what have they done to you?'

He unlocked the lounge and I swear that that spotted monstrosity jumped clear from the lounge, through the hall window and onto my chest. Down I went on the front lawn. Grrrr said Kong, several times.

'I'm very sorry' said the copper, 'but you're going to have to come with me.' I didn't believe he was sorry at all.

'All right,' I taunted. 'Come and get me!'

Well, nobody believed a word I said. Except the magistrate, who didn't believe that anyone could have invented such a tale. I was remanded for a couple of days, while they made enquiries, but then they caught up with cauliflower and his mate, so I was in the clear."

"Well," I said. "Poor old Frank. What a Bank Holiday!"

"You said it." He said, "next Bank Holiday Jenny and me are going away even if we have to walk home."

"Tell me," I asked, "Did he bite you badly?"

"Bite Me?"

"Yes - your hand." I pointed to the bandages.

"Oh," he said, "I did that backing out of the hall window. Nasty slice, went septic."

"Well he must have bitten you badly somewhere, to have kept you in bed for ten days."

I'm not in bed 'cause the dog bit me!" he shouted, opening his pyjamas. "Look, I've got *measles*!"

FLYING HORACE

A lot of people go to Jersey every year for their holidays. Among them, one year, was young Horace Naish and his family – Father, mother and sister Hermione.

They were rather lucky really because there had been a measles epidemic at Horace and Hermione's school, so it had broken up early for the summer holidays. That meant that they had been able start their holiday two weeks before everybody else in the country.

Now, Horace wasn't a bad boy, and on the other hand he wasn't a particularly good boy either. He was just a boy! And at this particular time he was having a bit of a feud with his sister. That's the way it is with brothers and sisters sometimes, they really get on each other's nerves and never miss a chance to wind each other up. And that's why the trouble started.

On the first morning of the holiday Horace made point of getting down for breakfast early. He knew that Hermione was going to have porridge for breakfast because they had all given their orders the previous night, so he emptied the sugar bowl and refilled it with salt from the other tables around. He reckoned that this was safe because no-one else in the family had porridge for breakfast and no-one took sugar in their tea.

Down came the rest of the family and the trouble started: although she's ordered it the night before Hermione now decided that she didn't want porridge, she wanted toast and marmalade, like everyone else. Dad, like dad's so often do, said that he would eat the porridge so that Hermione could have toast. This was very nice of him because he didn't really like porridge and that's why he put so much of what he thought was sugar on it.

He didn't really believe the first mouthful. In fact it wasn't until the third one went up and down his throat like a yo-yo that he got the message and ran out of the room with his napkin over his face.

Of course, the upshot of it all was that Horace was made to remain at the hotel while the rest of the family went out for a day of sea, sand, sunshine and ice creams.

For a while Horace slouched around the hotel. He tried reading the only book he could find in the lounge, which was called "Little Women" and gave up. He got bored playing with his yo-yo and wandered into the hotel kitchen. He was thrown out of there so tried out his new submarine spear gun. That was taken away by an angry manageress, after he had nearly shot the hotel cat!

After all that he got tired of trying to be a 'good' boy and sneaked out of the hotel by the back door. He spotted a bus marked "Zoo", so he jumped on, bought a ticket and sat back to enjoy the journey.

When he got there he found himself in another world. Quite apart from all the usual animals and birds, the lions and parrots and chimpanzees, there were lots of strange ones that Horace had never even heard of before, like pre-historic horses and something called an Aye Aye. Some of these were very rare in the wild and Mr Durrell, the man in charge of the zoo, had collected them so that he could save them from the extinction. But funnily enough, even though there were many strange and wonderful animals, what interested Horace most was a porridge-coloured pigeon that had got itself tangled in a bush. He didn't like the colour much because it reminded him of what happened to his father, but very carefully he disentangled it and for the rest of the day it followed him around like a pet dog.

It even followed him back to the hotel. He got back late, of course, and his father was so angry that he locked Horace in his bedroom. No lunch, nothing. And later, he saw the family all leave the hotel, cluttered with beach paraphernalia, like out of season Christmas trees.

So there was Horace, looking out of his window, feeling miserable and watching everybody else having a holiday. When up flew the porridge-coloured pigeon. It looked at him for a bit and then flew off. And it did it again and again, sailing to and fro outside Horace's window.

"It's all right for you," growled Horace, "flap and off you can fly."

"Well, so could you." Said the pigeon.

"Don't be ridiculous" said Horace, "what do you think I am, jet-propelled?"

"Don't need to be," said the pigeon, "you don't see great gusts of hot air coming out from under my tail do you? Only man would think of a way of making it all so difficult. The silliest little bird in the sky can fly; but man, who imagines that he's the cleverest creature in creation, can only do it with horses."

"Horses?" Said Horace.

"Well, horse-power – and whoever heard of a horse flying. Except a horse-fly, of course, but that's an entirely different entomological species!"

Needless to say, Horace didn't know what the pigeon was talking about, which might explain why he wasn't surprised that it was talking at all. "But people can't fly", he said.

"They can." Said the pigeon. "It's just a question of finding the right bird to teach you how. There aren't many of us but I'm one that can" and the pigeon flew into the room. "Now," it said, "get on the bed, lie flat on your back, put you hand on my tail and close your eyes."

Horace did as he was told and waited. After a while he said "Nothing's happening."

"Nothing's happening!" said the pigeon. "Just open your eyes."

Horace opened his eyes. The ceiling was gone. Above him was just the sky. He looked down, there was no bed beneath him. In fact, nothing beneath him for what looked like miles, and then it was roofs and chimneys and spires, all laced together with ribbons of road, and further along there was the bright blue sea sandwiching the surf on to the golden sand. He rolled over onto his stomach.

"Whoops," said the pigeon. "Don't do that. Or at least, let go of my tail first, it's very tiring flying upside down and towing you at the same time!"

"*Can* I let go?" said Horace.

"Any time you want," said the pigeon. So Horace let go and before long he was wheeling and sailing and diving in the soft summer air. "Look," said the pigeon suddenly, "There's your family" he waved a wing at the beach.

"Oh," said Horace," we'd better not get too close in case they see me."

"Don't be silly," said the pigeon. "You know what you humans say: 'Seeing is believing'. They would never believe that you can fly, so they won't see it."

That sounded quite reasonable to Horace but they didn't have time to put it to the test because just then mother waded out of the water and the family started packing up. "I think we'd better go back" he said, "I hate to think what will happen if I'm not in my room when they get back." And by the time that the rest of the family came tumbling up the stairs and father unlocked Horace's door, he was back, lying on his bed looking as if nothing unusual had happened at all. "Had a good day?" he asked.

"Yes," said father, "it's lovely here and I hope that you're going to behave well enough to join us tomorrow."

"Oh, I will," said Horace. "I promise."

But he never had a chance because that night at dinner Horace felt awful. Really ill, and halfway through the meal he had to go to bed. He had a temperature of 103°.

The local Dr. was called who took one look at Horace and said "Hospital. He's got Measles."

"He can't have," said mother. "He's already had it."

"Well," said the Dr. "He's got it again." And sure enough, Horace's face looked like a poppy field. So off to hospital he went.

For a few days Horace was a very poorly little boy indeed. But the worst was soon over, although he had to stay in hospital right up to the end of the holiday.

As a matter of fact the family were surprised that he took it so well, though he did have a nice room to himself and plenty to read. What they didn't know, of course, was that every afternoon, when Horace had been left alone to sleep, even when he was very ill, his pigeon friend had called to take him out for a gentle flight into the fresh, warm air. "Do you the world of good" said the pigeon. And it did.

Everyone was delighted with how quickly he got better, but they got worried when, two days before they were due to leave Jersey, Horace became all seedy and miserable again. 'He's going to have a relapse' they thought.

Very gently and kindly they asked him what was the matter. To begin with Horace wouldn't tell them but in the end he burst out crying and said "my pigeon didn't come today'.

"Your pigeon, dear?" said mother.

"Yes, he takes me flying," said Horace.

Father didn't say anything, he just thought that measles must have gone inwards!

"Can you fly, Horace?" said Hermione.

"Yes," said Horace, "but only with my pigeon and he didn't come today."

"Yes, well, alright son, don't worry, we'll get you another one when we get back home. Don't forget, we'll all be home again the day after tomorrow," said father.

And that made Horace cry even more!

The next day Horace was still miserable, but the Doctor said that he was over the measles and was perfectly all right, so he could leave the hospital. So off they all went. But things were not all right, later that night the parents heard screaming coming from the children's room and, dashing in, they found Horace jumping up and down on Hermione shouting "I can fly, I can fly." When they'd separated the children father said, very calmly, "All right Horace – show us how you can fly."

"I can't," said Horace. "Not without my pigeon and I don't know what's happened to him."

"I see," said father. "And where did you meet this pigeon?"

"At the Zoo," said Horace.

"All right," said Dad. "Tomorrow, before we get the boat home we'll go and look for him. How's that?"

"Great!" said Horace.

But now," said dad, "no more of this flying nonsense. OK?"

"It's not nonsense," screamed Horace. "I did fly, every day."

"Yes dear," said mother. "Of course you did."

"Eh?" said father.

"Well, he probably did," said mother. "Anyway, let's all go to sleep now and you can show us your pigeon friend, at the zoo, tomorrow." And as she pushed father out of the room she hissed "Don't fuss dear – it's probably just something to do with the measles."

The next day they packed up ready for the trip home and went to the zoo. They searched everywhere, saw dozens of pigeons but none of them, according to Horace, was his pigeon.
They had almost given up hope when they saw Mr Durrell.

Horace went up to him and said "Excuse me, but when I was here a few days ago, there was a porridge-coloured pigeon who followed me around. We can't find him now."

"Well," said Mr Durrell, "that's not the best description of a bird that I've ever heard, but if he's not out here then he may be the one that's perched in the bird-house looking miserable. Come and have a look."

So the went. "That's him!" shouted Horace, pointing to a miserable looking, pale, pigeon, covered in bright dandelion spots. "What's the matter him?"

"We're really not sure," said Mr Durrell. "We've never seen anything like it before. But if he wasn't a pigeon, I'd say he had measles."

THE BELLE OF THE BALL

I was beat. I don't mind telling you, I was proper flaked. And the Duke just about finished me off with his party idea. I could have crowned him with his own coronet!

"Really" he said, "You people have been so charming, such good company, we simply must have a farewell party."

Mark you, if I'd made the money that our company had paid for the loan of his castle and grounds, I'd have had Champagne flowing from the fountains.

You see, I was production manager on "Knights, Squires and Dames", one of those costume epics everyone was making a few years back. And we'd shot all the English location at the Duke's place. It was a wonderful place all right and looked smashing on film; but by the time I'd had five weeks of laying on costumes, suits of armour, horses, bows and arrows, lances and lunch wagons for five hundred mixed crowd, 23 bit players, fourteen leading characters and seven stars, this farewell party idea, properly put the wind up my farthingale!

The idea was that everybody should go in the costume they had been wearing for the film, and a few hundred odd locals were going to join in, in whatever they could muster. Oh a lovely idea! Everybody was for it, except me and the Wardrobe Department; they were in the same boat as I was: none of us had had a decent night's sleep since the location started, trying to keep tabs on everything, and one more night of it felt like one night too long.

Of course, everybody looked 'spoil-sport' at us. The stars fancied themselves with the local gentry, the feature players walked around talking like gentlemen farmers, and the extras were so keen on the idea that they even agreed to go to the party without asking for extra pay for wearing costumes. I thought that I was on a good thing there when I told them that they weren't going to be paid at all. But they said that that was all they could expect from a nasty, narrow-minded, mingy production manager, and they'd go in spite of me.

So, the party was on. And I must admit that on the night I felt a bit of a thrill myself. The castle seemed to come alive, like an orchard after a long winter. The great chandeliers in the ballroom sprouted wax blossoms, flame tipped, and in the candlelight and the costumes everyone looked beautiful: the Lords, the Ladies, and the commoners. All beautiful. Even the moguls from Wardour Street didn't look bad with visors covering up most of their faces.

The thrill wore off after a bit though, and I soon began to feel all caved-in again. I couldn't go to bed: I'd been given a room off the main hall and now they were using it as a ladies' retiring room. Bit silly really - none of the ladies wanted to retire half as much as I did!

So after an hour or so I took myself out into the rose-garden and stretched out on one of the benches. It was a beautiful night, full of stars with only a little rim of music round the castle to tell you where they left off and the lights began. Roses moved gently over my head, waltzing with a warm breeze, and the scent of them was like the caress of a warmly remembered love.

'Romantic isn't it?' I thought to myself. 'All you need is the right girl and you'd be away. Not far away, in your state of health, but showing willing.'

And then I noticed her for the first time, the girl. I don't know how long she'd been standing there in the arbour. She just seemed to grow out of the roses. Looked like one too; a slender white rose, stemmed on a dress of velvet green that fell in folds at her feet. Her blue-black hair, framed close to her face, faded off into the night sky.

"Hello," I said, "Where did you spring from?"

"I have been here a long time, sir," she replied.

"Well, you can cut out the 'Sir' bit," I said. "The picture's over now. Nice job the wardrobe did on you with that dress. Don't know what period they think it is, but it's a nice job. Funny I can't remember it; which sequence were you in: the banquet or the jousting? Or were you in the bathing shots? None of the girls wore much in those." I was trying to sound nice and warm and wolfy - after all, how tired can you get? But she choked me off very sharpish;

"I think sir, you mistake me," she said. "I am of the house, not of your party."

"Oh, one of the guests, are you?"

"No sir, not one of the guests, I am the lady of the house."

Well, of course, that put me right back where I belonged. As a matter of fact, I didn't even know that the Duke was married, but I wouldn't have blamed him anyway for keeping his wife out of the way while our particular chaos was going on. I started apologising all over again, but she stopped me and then apologised for disturbing me!

"Perhaps sir, I had better leave you to your slumbers?" she said.

"Oh no," I said, "I'm wide awake now; in any case, I was only resting. It's a lovely garden, isn't it?"

"Would you like to see more of it," she asked. "Come, I will show you my favourite places." She went ahead of me. At times she seemed almost to dissolve into the green of the garden and the deep purple of the night. She stopped first at a little pool fed by a trickling fountain that cut a passage of light in the dark water, through which goldfish flicked on and off like strips of neon. She knelt by the pool and I stood over her; for a while we stayed like that, still in the quiet night, just watching. Then she gave me her hand to help her up, and as we walked across the lawn she left it in mine. Once, she stumbled a little and my arm went round her to save her from falling. For a moment she lay quiet against me and I saw that her eyes were the colour of the night sky, and there were stars in them. Gently, she moved away and took my hand again as we walked towards the castle. Our fingers linked and the palms of our hands met like doves.

Music was still coming from the castle as we got closer, though the quality of it seemed to have changed somehow. But then this girl had changed the whole quality of the night for me. It didn't seem to matter that she was a duke's wife; that we were walking, star-struck, into the Duke's home; that not a word had been spoken since we began to walk. It didn't even matter that this could spell trouble; that this was just the very kind of thing that the company relied on me to see didn't happen when our units went on location, and blood began to run a bit hot with the locals. It wasn't that I didn't care about the consequences of what I was doing, there just didn't seem to be any question of consequences. There was no grand passion or reckless emotion; it was almost as if I was doing something that had all been done before, and had to be done again.

We went through the heavy metalled door and into the candle-lit hall. The ballroom lay off to our left, and through the open doors the music rose and fell with gusts of laughter and chatter. We could see the dancers milling around in a smoky kaleidoscope of colour. We stood looking for a moment. Nobody took any notice of us. Then she turned and smiled at me and shook her head. Before I could make any sort of answer I found myself trailing up the broad, oak staircase behind her. At the top she pulled me back into the shadows, and from there we looked down into the well of noise below us.

"Shouldn't we join in?" I said.

She giggled. Now a giggle isn't the most romantic noise at the best of times, and it was only then that I realised she wasn't all that much more than a child. "No, please," she said, "I am in no mood for company." It was this odd, dignified way of talking that she had that made her seem older than her years. "Have you yet been shown the View Balcony?" she went on.

"No," I said, "what's that?"

"Come, I will show you. It is said that from it one can see the whole of our estates and only when the eye fails is the land no longer the Duke's."

We turned off the corridor into a long, unlit room. She led me swiftly through it. There couldn't have been any furniture or at the rate we were going we'd have fallen over it.

"What's this place?" I asked, as we went.

"The picture gallery," She replied. "Have you not been shown it?"

"No," I said, "not shown it exactly, I believe that I walked through it months ago, when we were checking the location."

"How very remiss of the Duke. You must see it in particular. I will take you to it by day."

"You'll have to hurry," I said, "we're not here much longer."

She stopped short and I nearly walked into her. She turned and in the darkness I could feel her looking at me, though I couldn't see a thing myself. "No," she said, "not much longer." She sounded sad, which was a bit odd, I thought, seeing that she'd kept out of our way all the time we'd been at the castle. But I didn't think anything long, for her hold on my hand tightened and suddenly I felt her breath on my cheek and a touch like the fall of pollen on my lips. And I hardly had time to register this before she was leading me swiftly on again.

At the end of the gallery we went through a small door, into a little boudoir of a room, one whole wall of which was taken up by big French windows. These too we went through, and then there we stood, out in the open again, under a night sky pinned up with stars.

The dark land rolled away below us, striped with streams running at the feet of hills which wore woods like ragged fur coats. And for the first time I envied the Duke. We stood without speaking; her hand moved along my arm and I envied the Duke more. This time the envy was almost a pain. I took her by the shoulders and crushed her into my arms, as though I was trying to make her feel some of my pain and as I felt her small bones moving under my hands her mouth petalled open under my lips.

So we stood. Maybe a second; maybe a minute; but all of a life-time.

The first I knew of the man who tore us apart was when I felt his hand grooving into my arm. Then I saw a thin face, with blazing green eyes under heavy black hair as he hurled me down into the corner of the balcony. He seemed to have maniacal strength for, taking the girl by the throat, he lifted her bodily and with one movement threw her over the parapet. She made no sound. The night air ripped at her clothes as she fell, but that was all. The dark man turned and as he swirled back into the little room, I got the impression of a riding outfit under his cloak.

It's easy enough to write it all down now; tidily and in order, but it couldn't have taken more than a split second to happen, and he was gone before the full understanding and horror of what had happened, hit me.

I struggled to my feet. I felt sick and dazed as I staggered off the balcony, through the little room and into the long, dark, picture gallery. I knew that I would never find the door in the darkness, so I stood there shouting for help. Shouting 'Murder' to the empty room, with the sound of music in my ears.

For all the music, somebody must have heard me, for I remember the door at the end of the gallery bursting open and the lights going on. Then I passed out cold on the floor.

I came to with the Duke's arm supporting me, and the First Assistant throwing water in my face - he'd been wanting to do something like that ever since the picture started! I looked around the faces bending over me, then the horror came back. "Murder!" I said. "It was murder..."

"Yes, old boy," said the Duke. "Now, take it easy and we'll have you tucked up in bed in no time. You've been over doing it a bit, that's all."

"No," I said, "there's been a murder..." and I was trying to tell them who had been murdered as they helped me to my feet. As I came upright, the gallery came into perspective and on the wall, straight in front of me, two full-length portraits looked down at me. One was of a girl, stemming like a white rose from a velvet, green dress that fell in folds at her feet; and the other was of a dark, green-eyed man, wearing a cloak over an old-fashioned riding outfit. I stared at the pictures and everyone went quiet around me: "Who are they?" I croaked.

"That's my great, grand uncle and his wife," said the Duke. "Great tragedy there. The story is that he suspected her of associating with some theatrical vagabond. They had a shocking quarrel and he rode off to London, in a filthy temper, leaving her behind. She, poor girl, in a fit of despair, threw herself off of the balcony. They didn't find her 'till the next day and then it took days more to find uncle.

Terrible business for him, poor devil. He never got over it. Never married again. In fact, it's said that he became quite disturbed. Now old boy, come along, time you were in bed. You'll feel better after a good night's sleep."

THE GREAT TRAIN ROBBERY

I went to the Cup Final a few years ago. First time I'd ever been, and I had a great time. A friend of mine who's mad on the game had a ticket, and then got Mumps two days before the match, so he gave it to me.

Mark you, it wasn't a good start: I found myself standing behind a bloke who was about 6 ft. square, and I spent the first couple of minutes guessing what was happening from the changing colour of his neck!

Of course, I kept dodging from side to side, to try and see the pitch, but every time I swung to the right my shoulder cannoned into what couldn't have been higher than the third waistcoat button of the biggest man I've ever seen. He made the chap in front of me look as if he never happened.

After about the third shove he looked down at me and said "Y'know I could have you disqualified for bumping and boring."

"Oh, I'm sorry," I said, "I should have brought a periscope..."

He looked at me and then at the bloke in front. "Come on sonny," he said, "change places with me." 'SONNY'!! Me! - I hadn't been called that for thirty years, but I changed, gratefully, and had a great view from then on.

Well, the match went on and we didn't take any more notice of each other until half-time, when he offered me a fag and I swapped him a piece of orange. And then at the end of the match we pushed our way out together - well anyway, he pushed and I just drifted along in his wake. And so we landed outside Wembley.

"Come on lad," he said, "I reckon we could do with a cup of tea after that."

"Yes," I said, "us and 90,000 others!"

"Don't worry," he said, "I know a place just round the back of here."

So off we went. The 'place round the back' was really the front room of a private house, where a couple of old dears picked up a bit of spending money a couple of times a year by providing tea and cakes after a big match. "You must have been exploring this area for years to find this place," I said.

"Aye," he said, "I've been living round here since the fifties, but I haven't missed many Cup Finals ever since I was old enough to travel to them. There was one though, just after the war that was.... but...."

"But what?"

"But that's a longer story than you want to hear on an afternoon like this."

"You'd be surprised," I said, "Try me."

"Well," he said, "in those days, Bert Allison and me were pals, real pals; went everywhere, did everything together; even wore the same kind of clothes: I remember that year we bought two Harris Tweed jackets, both same colour and design. 'The hairy Monsters' they used to call us - we were about the same size. Every year we went to the Cup Final. Didn't matter who was playing, we went. We took it in turns to get the tickets, this time Bert had got them, right struggle he'd had too. Then, it's early Spring of course, I started courting. I'll never forget his face when I told him. He had called for me at home. I was shaving."

"What are you shaving for Jack?" He said.

"Unyuh huh - huh - huh unyuh." I replied.

"Oh," he said. "Gerraway! Come on, hurry up or we'll never get a table at the club."

"Umlah hgnot umgoosnooker."

"What 'd you say?"

I stopped shaving. "I'm not going to play snooker," I said.

"All right then, we'll go to the flicks if you like."

"That's what I'm doing," I said.....

"Fair enough, we'll ...."

"With Elsie." I went on.

"Elsie?!"

"Yes."

"Elsie 'oo?'"

"Elsie Crumb," I said.

"You mean that kid who was at school with us, with pigtails and a mouth full of railway lines?"

"Give over," I said, "that was seven years ago."

"I don't care how long ago it was," he said. "She was a little so-and-so then and by now she's had time to develop!"

"But she's changed Bert," I said, "after all, she was sent to London to be finished."

"Finished!" he said, "Pity she was ever started!"

Well, a bit more of that sort of thing and Bert and me ended up having a right, royal row. In the end my dad came up to us: "'ere," he said, "if you're going to argue like that, you'd better put that razor down!"

I didn't see Bert for about a week, and then I had to go and look for him down at the Working Men's club. He was playing snooker with Harry Ramsay. "Hello, Bert," I said.

"Quiet on the shot please," said Harry, as Bert went in off the black. "That's seven away; leaves you wanting a snooker, Bert."

"Look Bert," I said, "I only wanted to say...."

" 'Aven't you said enough?" said Bert, "You cost me seven points every time you open your mouth!"

"I'm sorry," I said, "I only wanted to say that you needn't worry about the tickets for the Final, I'll take 'em both."

"Oh you will, will you?" he said.

"Yes. Elsie wants to go."

"Oh she does, does she?"

"Look," I said, "are you going to sell me those tickets or not?"

"You're joking," he said, "You couldn't get those tickets from me even if it was for your uncle in Hire Purchase - and Heaven knows, I'm far enough behind on my payments!"

I told Elsie that night.

"Oh," she said, in a posh voice with icicles dripping from it, "I thought that Herbert was supposed to be a friend of yours." She spoke like that ever since she'd been finished.

"Well of course he's a friend of mine. But there are some things....."

"Well, if I was in love with someone, and that someone wanted something very much, and I knew someone who had that something and said he was my friend, I should either get that something from that someone for that other someone, or never call him a friend of mine again!"

We were sitting on the settle in her front parlour, and I stayed quiet for a minute or two, working it all out. Then: "To tell you the truth," I said, "that's what I have done."

"I suppose you think that's clever," she said, "where on earth do you think you can get a Cup Final ticket now?!"

"But you just said I should never call him a friend of mine again!"

"Oh, now I suppose you're going to say that I'm the kind of girl that comes between a man and his best friend." And she started sobbing.

Now I didn't know if I was coming or going. "Nay, Elsie," I said, "don't cry love, don't cry. No. There, there - I'll tell you what we'll do: we'll take the day trip to London anyway. It doesn't matter about the old Cup Final. We can have a lovely time seeing the sights and we can go to a show or something and catch the last train back."

She snorted loudly into the handkerchief I gave her, and reluctantly agreed.

So crack of dawn on Cup Final day, all dressed up in my new Harris Tweed jacket, I called for Elsie.

"She's in the bath." Her mother said.

"We've got a train to catch," I said. "What did she want to bath this morning for?"

Her mother gave me a cup of tea and a dirty look. "My Elsie baths *every* morning," she said. So I shut up.

Well we missed the first two specials and the third one was just about to pull out as we got on to the platform. I went running up the station, dragging Elsie behind me, and pulled open a carriage door just as the train began to move. I chucked her in and ended up sitting on the floor

- well, I thought I was on the floor until a fat lady who was sitting in the left-hand corner leant over and said "Young man, you're sitting on our Willie!" She was right. Willie was about three months old, in a carry cot down at her feet, and as I got up he started screaming fit to bust.

Then I noticed that Elsie, still trying to get her hat out of her eyes, was sitting on some feller's lap in the other corner. I couldn't see who it was, 'cause she was all over him, but I suddenly caught a glimpse of a Harris Tweed jacket half hung off the rack; and I knew who it was alright. "Bert Allison," I said, "move over and let the lady sit down."

He sort of came up for the third time. "Oh," he said. "It's you.'"

"That's right," I said. "Let the lady sit down."

"She is sitting down, isn't she?" He said, and Elsie giggled - she'd got her hat straight by now.

"You know what I mean," I said, "I don't want any trouble with you."

"No trouble at all," he said, and he stood up and made a big bow to Elsie, bumping into me as he did it. Just then the train swung and down I went, onto the same fat lady's lap. There was a terrible howl: "Young man..." she said, "I know," I said, "I'm sitting on our Willie."

In the end we all got settled. It was right hot in that carriage, so I took off my jacket and tossed it up on the rack. I was sitting between the fat lady and our Willie on one side, and three very thin men in black suits and bowlers on the other. Elsie was sitting next to Bert in the corner on the other side.

"Alexander," she said, - she never called me Alec - "you do look odd, sitting about in your braces."

"Maybe he'd look odder without them," said Bert, who was wearing a belt. I took them off. Then, without saying a word, I took my tie off and tied it round the top of my trousers.

"Quiet, aren't you." said Bert. "Why don't you introduce me to the lady?"

"You know her well enough," I said.

"Just as well too," said Elsie, "Wouldn't have been very nice sitting on a stranger's lap, would it?"

"Well I'm glad you found it nice on mine," said Bert.

Elsie started to giggle. "Oh you".... then she caught my eye ... "know what I mean." She finished.

"You bet I do," Bert said.

Then the thin man next to me saw the funny side of it. His face didn't change but he began shaking up and down and making a noise like a collector's box on a flag day. Sitting next to him it was like being massaged by a skeleton.

"You going to a funeral?" I said. And he stopped laughing.

"No," he said, "we're going to London for a bit of fun."

At that moment the ticket collector came in, and we all started fishing around. Bert got his wallet out of his jacket and handed over his ticket. Elsie peeked into the wallet and said "Ooh, are those Cup Final tickets?" Bert took his ticket back from the collector, snapped it into his wallet and shoved it back into his jacket. "That's right," he said. "Never seen one before?"

"No," she said, "and not likely to again."

"Oh, aren't you going to the match then?" said Bert. Rubbing it in.

"No, Alexander couldn't find any tickets," she said.

By now I could see that that this was going to be a lovely trip; but the worst part came when we were nearly in London: the fat lady had given our Willie a bottle full of milk, and what with his wrappings and his empty bottle and him, she didn't know which to put down first.

"Help the lady, Alexander," said Elsie. He wasn't a moment in my arms before he started screaming the place down.

"Put him over your shoulder and pat his back," said the fat lady, so I did. Suddenly there was a little gulp and he stopped crying. "There," she said, "you'll make a proper dad - he's brought up his wind."

Then the back of my shirt began to feel damp. "He's brought up more than just his wind," I said. "Excuse me." And I stood up. As I bent over to lay Willie back in her lap, I suddenly felt the tie round my waist slipping. Well, it was a question of dropping the baby or.... and after all, you can't go bouncing babies round railway carriages, can you? Of course, everybody was roaring with laughter - the three thin men sounded like a fleet of bicycles being ridden through a bead curtain - but not Elsie. There was a nasty glint in her eye and she looked very hard the other way as I pushed past, out into the corridor.

In the little room at the end of the corridor, I'd just about got my shirt off and was cleaning up, when I heard voices I recognised, outside:

"Oh come on now, surely he wouldn't mind you having a cup of coffee with me, if that's what you're worried about."

"I am not in the least worried about what Alexander thinks," replied Elsie. "It's just that he's so stupid and clumsy."

"Ay," said Bert. "He's a bit of a gumph."

"Whatever he is," she said, "it no longer concerns me."

"You're going to have quite a day, aren't you?"

"Oh it's going to be dreadful! No Cup tickets, no nothing, just walking around."

"Well, I've got *two* tickets. You could always come with me."

"Oh I...." Elsie paused.... "Well why not?"

I didn't hear any more, as they continued on their way to the buffet car. But I'd heard plenty. Nobody talked to anybody for the rest of the journey, and as we drew into London Elsie said "Alexander, I have to go to the chemists. If you will go to the buffet, I will meet you there."

So that was it. Illusions never die easy, but it's just as well to catch them young. I didn't say anything. I just stood up, reached up to the rack, put on the jacket and went."

I finished up my tea. It was cold now. "Well?" I said.

"Well what?"

"Is that the end of the story?"

"Aye," he said, "That's all."

"Do you mean to say that you let Bert rob you of your girl and leave you with no friends, no tickets, no nothing, for a whole day in London?"

"What do you mean 'no tickets,' " he said. "That was Bert's jacket I put on.!"

BLOW YOUR WHISTLE MR LEVY

I was in the front room, finishing the trousers for Symington's, when Bessie said "So they don't get the trousers first thing in the morning. It won't kill them!"

Of course, she was right, like women are always right - half right - they've got no ethics, women. For years, even before the last war, I have been stitching trousers for Symington's, and always, when I have said they would have them, they have had them. That meant something to me. It meant something to my boy Davey, God rest him, when he was working with me in the front room, though he didn't work with me for very long.

I remember saying to him "All right Davey, but why the air force? I don't like these flying machines, Davey," I said, "Why the air force?"

"Because they want chaps who know about radio, dad," he replied.

And he was right. He knew about radio. More even than he knew about stitching. But Anne? (such trouble if I call her Hannah!) Like her mother again; "Why do you do it dad?" she used to say from a little girl. "Stitch, stitch, stitch, 'till your eyes go in and out like the needle. And what for? For Symington's. Why not get a cutter and stitch for yourself? You could find all the customers you want."

Maybe she was right at that. But I don't know. Somehow, when you're making a living, and the children are growing up, you feel you can't gamble with their future while it is their future. 'Later on', you think. And then comes 'later on', and you're a bit older and you feel a bit tireder in the evenings. Too tired to start worrying about finding cutters and customers. And so you carry on stitching for Symington's, and maybe you could have done worse.

So when Bessie said "Don't be too long, Morry," I said "All right." I knew that I'd be two more hours, but the cold fish that Bessie was taking to her sister's, for our supper, wouldn't get any colder. And Bessie and her sister didn't need me there to help them talk, anyway.

Then the front door slammed. And soon came that nice quiet, full of little noises, like the needle pricking, my breathing, the tick of the clock that Bessie's sister gave us for our Silver Wedding; noises that go round the quiet like a frame goes round a picture, and cuts a little piece out from the world.

Sometimes when it's like that I know Davey is there with me. We don't say anything. It's nice he should come at all to be with me, so what should I say? But the work gets done so much quicker when he's there. Always he was a good worker, my Davey.

He was with me the evening I am telling about, but he didn't stay long because soon I had to get off the bench and do the blackout, and what with walking sticks and chairs and curtain rings, it's a noisy business and upsets everything.

When I had done the blackout I couldn't, somehow, get on with the stitching again and I was beginning to feel hungry already. I began to think like Bessie said: "So they don't get them first thing" - and if they say anything, I can tell them 'there's a war on'! For four years, every time I wanted one kind of cotton instead of another kind, baked potatoes instead of boiled potatoes, a packet of razor blades, a box of matches, somebody has said to me "Don't you know there's a war on, Mr Levy?" Don't I know! So now I couldn't say it to Symington's.

So I went out of the front room and down the couple of steps to the kitchen and put the kettle on. I thought "I'll have a cup of tea and a piece of cake and then I'll be able to settle down and work again, and Bessie won't miss me for another half an hour or so, anyway."

The kettle was just about on the boil when I heard the buzz-bomb. It didn't seem very near and I poured some hot water into the teapot to warm it, and then emptied it away into the sink.

It was louder now, the bomb.

I put the pot on the gas stove and walked to the kitchen door. Opposite was the cupboard under the stairs that lead up to the bedrooms. The gas and electricity and water mains were there, and I had had the cupboard made stronger for us to sit in while there was the blitz. And I'd put some matches and a candle and a flask of water in there. But we didn't use it for a long time now.

The bomb sounded different to all the others I had heard. Even the ones that had gone right over our roof hadn't sounded like this. The noise was so loud now that it wasn't really a noise any more. It was a strength that could move things. It shook all the cups and saucers off the dresser, sent the kitchen table sliding over to the fireplace till it hit against the fender and stayed there shivering and jerking like a frightened horse.

It pressed on my ears until I thought my head must burst like a walnut, when you squeeze the crackers too hard. Then it went off and must have blown me across the hall into the cupboard. But how, I don't remember. All I can remember was a big, singing redness in my head and thinking I must be blind because only darkness came when the red faded.

Like a blind man I put out my arms and reached forward until my hands touched something. I pushed and it moved. I felt round the shape of it. It was a chair, one of the wooden chairs we had put in the cupboard, and the seat was level with my waist.

Suddenly I was afraid like I had never been before.

"Even if you are alive," I thought, "do you want to go on living with no legs? Bessie hasn't got enough trouble she should have you to nurse and push around in a wheelchair always?"

I could feel the sweat prickling through my skin and rolling down my face. "Dear God," I prayed, "please, better let me die. If I am blind, well, I am blind. But crippled too? Better I should die, dear God!"

And I waited to die.

I think I waited a long time, and while I waited I could feel myself getting tighter inside, like a little ball of madness was rolling itself up in my stomach and forcing itself up through my throat until it rushed out of my mouth. And there in the darkness I screamed at God to let me die and threw myself across the chair and beat my head on the wooden seat and pressed down on it with my hands. Then, even in my madness, I felt my legs. As I pushed on the seat of the chair, so I felt my legs move. There was something holding them but as I pulled, they moved.

I stopped screaming. And I wasn't mad any more. Slowly, I tried to turn my legs. First one, then the other. And they both moved and I could hear the pieces of brick and rubble shift and slide down and settle again when I stopped moving them. "Gently," I thought. "There's no need to hurry. You've got plenty of time. Your legs won't be of much use to you if you pull the house in on top of yourself with them."

So I could stand! And I was crying - a grown man, and I was crying. I laughed at myself and I couldn't stop laughing. And I laughed and I cried because I couldn't stop crying either. So for a while I sat there laughing and crying until I could think again, and started to work things out.

Over my head, when I stood up, I could feel the cupboard ceiling going up in steps, and the extra heavy beams we had put in, going up with them. And behind me was the shelf I had put there three years ago. Yes, I knew where I was all right, but where the door of the cupboard had been was like a wall now. The whole house had come down over the staircase and I was under it!

As easy as that!

Now, as I try to tell how this happened to me, it all seems so simple. Maybe I'm making a fuss about nothing. But it isn't as easy as that really. That isn't all that happens. When the madness stops and the roaring goes out of your head, first there's peace and quiet like when you've dodged out of a gale into a shelter on the sea-front: all that salty wind that was blowing into your mouth and nose and beating on the drums of your ears is turned off, like with a switch. Then one by one, your senses come back. You begin to hear again. Water dripping; little noises like mice pattering all around you, except when the beams over your head groan loud, like a tired old man, then even the mice noises stop, like they were holding their breath and waiting - just like you.

Smells begin to mean something again. The thick dust over your tongue and your nostrils smells sour like builders' plaster when it is still wet. There is the smell of something scorched, something damp and dying, and the smell of gas. The taste in your mouth is sharp - like you've eaten cakes with too much soda in them, and little pieces of grit grind on you teeth every time you close your jaws.

Yes, you're coming back to life again. Even the darkness isn't so black any more. You're coming alive because these things mean you're alive. And you begin to feel afraid because dying is still in front of you - burnt, suffocated, drowned crushed or gassed - these are the ways people die now.

You understand? I am trying to tell you how my mind was working. All these things were beating around in my head like butterflies, each one resting for a second on my brain and chewing a piece away like it was a cabbage, until suddenly one of the butterflies was caught and my brain hung on to it: I needn't be gassed! Why should I be gassed when all I had to do was find the mains tap on the wall behind me. And just like that, now that I could think about one thing, I could think about everything: the water could be turned off as well, and the electricity. There was air enough for some time anyway, and because something was scorched, did I have to burn to death?

Yes, I could think clearly again: if I stood up from where I was sitting I had to stoop a little to my left; I could stand straight up to my right, but where the stairs came down to the floor I would have to bend nearly double. This much was easy to work out.

So I stood up from the chair, stooping a little, and banged my head on the shelf that I had put there three years ago! I sat down on the chair and laughed. But this time it was all right to laugh. "Such a clever fellow you are, Morry," I thought. "Always you think of everything but what's right on top of you!" But even a bump on the head can be useful: now I remembered the water and the candle and the whistle and the matches, all on the shelf.

So I got up again, moving forward as I did, and turned to my right, bending down low and feeling along the wall for the mains taps. I squatted to turn them off, and like that I worked my way backwards until my back was pressed against the wall of rubble and fallen wood, then I eased along until I could feel the chair in front of me again, and stood up, stooping just a little as my head pressed against one of the beams I had put in to strengthen the stairs. Opposite me now, about level with my chest, was the shelf, and more than anything else at that moment I wanted the flask that was tucked away where the shelf was nailed to the stairs. I found it. It was heavy and full. I put both my hands round it and carefully lifted it towards me. It came up suddenly light in my hands and water gushed out, splashing on the shelf and down the front of my trousers. For a minute I stood like that with the flask in my hand. I couldn't understand what had happened. Then I felt under the flask. There was no bottom to it, just a sharp, clean edge where the blast had cut through it like with a diamond.

You know how it is when you have something extra special nice to do, like a picnic on Sunday that you've looked forward to for a whole week, in the summer? And every day of the week gets more easy to bear, even though the needle is wet between your fingers and the sweat stings in your eyes as you bend over the cloth, because every day that comes is the day after one is gone and one day nearer Sunday? Then comes Sunday and you are up early and the sky is grey. When you leave home it is drizzling. The train is crowded, the sandwiches are hard, the lettuce is soft, the jelly wasn't set and has spilled on the cake, and when you are in the middle of an open field there is a cloudburst. You know how it is?

Well that's how I felt. Only with those things, later on you can laugh. With this, I shall never laugh. I was angry. Angry and weak, like a baby with a toy just in front of him and he can only crawl backwards. Angry and bitter that my life should be such a toy - dangled in front of me, but just so's I shouldn't reach it.

So I put the broken flask on the shelf and began to feel for the candle and the matches. Soon, I found them. I knew that the whole place might blow up if I struck a match, and if it didn't blow up, the candle would still burn up the air. But I was sure now that I was meant to die. There would be darkness enough then. Now I was tired of the darkness, I wanted to see.

Yes - fine and brave and angry I was - but somehow I was glad when I struck the match and it lit, and I could see, and nothing blew up.

It's funny how candles always make things look cosy. I remember when Davey mended the fuse for the first time; and after, for two nights, we had candles, while the man from the builders put new wires everywhere, everything looked nicer, just old and comfortable, not shabby like in the electric light. The same now. As the light from the candle got stronger and pushed the darkness away into the corners, things didn't look so bad anymore. I was alive, and it was a pleasure to be alive.

The first thing I saw in the light from the candle was the bottom of the flask, like a saucer, and it was full of water. This time I could see and I made no mistakes. I pulled it gently to the edge of the shelf and sipped at it. The first little mouthful I rinsed my mouth with and spat out. It was good to feel my mouth clean again. Then I tilted the saucer and drank a mouthful; and then it was all gone. The bottom of a flask, like with a bottle, is punched up in the middle, so two little mouthfuls and it was all gone. Still, my mouth was clean, I wasn't thirsty any more and a candle is a cheerful thing. Yes, it was a pleasure to be alive again.

Until I looked at the hook where the whistle should have been hanging. It was empty! At first I didn't believe it, and I felt all round the hook with my fingers, but there was nothing wrong with my eyes, the whistle wasn't there. I moved the candle up and down the shelf: where it was dark, under the stairs; and where it was open and light. Then I felt all over the shelf, but the whistle wasn't there. I'd forgotten all about it until I saw that empty nail and then suddenly it meant everything. That's how you keep alive when you are buried under a house: from one hope to a new hope you climb and climb, up towards life. And when there is no new hope to climb to, then you begin to die.

And I wanted to live now. I wanted to find that whistle and blow so the world should know: I am here. Morry Levy is alive!

I took the candle and looked on the floor under the shelf. I pushed my hands through the bits of brick and plaster. Where the water had mixed with them they spread like mud all over the floor. The whistle wasn't there. When I got off my hands and knees I was out of breath, so I sat on the chair and made myself rest and think. Like one of Davey's sums from school, I thought. "It's no use rushing at it dad," he used to say. "You've got to work it out by logic." Logic. So all right, logic! Like Davey said. He always got his sums right, maybe this time it would work for me. So I started to work it out: If the blast had blown straight on to the whistle it would have pushed it further on to the nail, not off it; but if it had blown against the wall and then hit the whistle from the other side, the blast would have blown it over towards the door of the cupboard, then the rubble would have fallen on it and trapped it in the doorway.

Crazy logic? Maybe. But it was right. I dug into the rubble on the floor where the door had been, right in front of the nail. Like a dog I dug, and a dozen things I held to the candle: a piece of the kitchen stove; a teaspoon blown like an 's'; things I couldn't recognise at all; and then I found it! The whistle. Not silvery anymore, and the mouthpiece wrapped over the drum part like a piece of paper.

I fixed the candle back on the shelf and sat on the chair, looking at the twisted whistle in my hand. I was more out of breath than ever and could feel the sweat trickling down the back of my knees. And somehow, although I sat quiet now, for a long time, looking at the whistle, I was still hot and it wasn't getting any easier to breath. Then I knew, it wasn't digging for the whistle that made me out of breath, or being excited finding it, it was the air; it wasn't very good any more.

I looked hard at everything. This was all of my home that I had left to look at, maybe for the last time, after twenty years. So I looked hard at everything. And then I reached up and snuffed out the candle.

For a long time I sat very still and quiet so I should get cool again and breath easier. Then I began to straighten the whistle with my fingers. The mouthpiece had been beaten over like with a hammer. When I could get my fingers under it, it came up easy, but I had to go very slow for fear I should snap it off altogether as I bent it straight. By the time I had it straight enough I was sweating hot again and hadn't the breath to give it a good blow, so I rested again.

I don't know what I expected to happen when I did blow it. Maybe the walls would fall down like Jericho, and I would walk straight out into the street. Or a way would be cut for me like for Moses through the Red Sea. Anyway, something should happen. But nothing did. The whistle was stuffed full of dirt and brick dust and it nearly fell out of my hand, so hard I blew it, but it didn't make a sound. I dug the nails of my left hand - there weren't any left on my right - into the hole in the drum part and loosened some of the muck that was caked up in there, and some of it came out when I knocked the whistle against the chair. But it felt to me like I was knocking with a twenty pound hammer, so heavy such a little whistle felt.

After I rested some more I tried it again. This time there was a noise. It wasn't sharp and clear, it was just a kind of high, bubbling noise. Like a boy blowing down his bubble pipe into soapy water to make it lather. I tried blowing much harder and heard the blood roaring in my head louder than the whistle, and saw little lights dancing in front of my eyes. And then I lay back in the chair panting like a dog on a hot day. I leant my head back against the wall and felt myself crying a little. I didn't want to cry. At this moment I didn't feel afraid any more. My head hurt and it was hard to breath, but I didn't feel afraid. It was just that I hadn't got strength to make myself do or not do anything any more. And so I felt the tears running with the sweat down my face and I just couldn't help it.

"Mr Levy."

'Yes' I thought, 'it's a good name; a lot of people have got it; blackguards, heroes and pages in the 'phone book of ordinary ones like you.'

"Mr Levy."

Yes. Mr Levy. Always there'll be somebody, somewhere, calling 'Mr Levy', but they won't mean you any more, Morry.

"Blow your whistle Mr Levy."

No, I wasn't hearing things in my head. I wasn't crazy. The words were real. Faint, but quite clear. Somebody was calling.

I couldn't answer for a minute. There were so many things I wanted to say and they all tried to come out together, so I could feel my lips moving but nothing came out. Then: "Who's that?" I called back. My voice sounded loud in the little cupboard.

"It's me ... Mrs Arnold...Mrs Arnold next door."

She didn't have to tell me from where. Poor Mrs Arnold, millions of people she might have been bombed with, and it had to be me! For twenty years she lives next door, and for nineteen years, eleven months and thirty days we only hear from her by little notes: 'Would the children not climb over her fence for their ball.' 'Would Bessie not feed scraps to her cat.' 'Would Davey make less noise with his motor bike.'

The only day I ever spoke to Mrs Arnold was the first day we moved in. We got to the house late in the evening and by the time the furniture was taken off the van it was too late to buy milk for a cup of tea. So I knocked at her door and asked did she have a little milk to spare? She looked at me, up and down - you know, you don't look so good when you've just moved a houseful of furniture - and then "No." she said, "I have no milk to spare." And shut the door.

Well, maybe she didn't have any milk to spare. Maybe all she had was a drop for breakfast and that wouldn't have been any good for me anyway. Maybe lots of things. But now it didn't matter what had passed. Now we were just two people very near to being dead. "Are you all right, Mrs Arnold?" I called.

"I can't move." She said.

"What happened?" I asked.

"I don't know properly," she said, "I was under the stairs and then there was the explosion. Something hit me across the back and I think I have been unconscious 'till now. And I can't move."

Now I knew that I didn't have to shout. Her voice was very faint, but not because of the wall between us, but just because she didn't have much strength left. "That's nothing to worry about, Mrs Arnold," I said. "I can't move much myself but they'll soon find us, I've got a whistle."

"Yes, I heard it," she said, blow it again, Mr Levy."

So I blew it as hard as I could, until my ears hurt and the lights came dancing back in front of my eyes.

"It doesn't sound very loud, Mr Levy." She said. And she was right, but what could I do?

"No, it's not very loud," I said. "They got whistles for when dogs are a long way off that don't make any sound at all, but the dogs hear them."

"Oh," she said, "well let's hope they got dogs digging for us."

And I knew I wasn't fooling her. And there wasn't any need to fool her because she was ready for whatever was coming and she wasn't afraid. "Mrs Arnold," I said, "it would have been nice to know you better."

"Thank you, Mr Levy." she said.

And then we talked. A whole twenty years' worth we talked. I told her about Davey and she told me about her sweetheart being killed in the last war; and I told her about how proud Hannah had been when she got a job with one of these ministries so she didn't have to stitch for Symington's any more, and found herself stitching parachutes all day. Yes, we talked.

I don't know how long we talked, but the spaces between talking began to get longer. Not because we'd finished all there was to be talked about, but just that it was getting harder to push the words out, and taking longer to get the breath to say the next words after the others had been said.

Every now and then, while we talked, Mrs Arnold would stop a while and ask me to blow the whistle again, and then we went on talking again, until now Mrs Arnold's voice hardly came through the wall, and when I blew the whistle it felt like a garden rake was being dragged up through my chest. "Perhaps we'd better not talk for a bit, eh, Mrs Arnold?" I said. "And if you want to know if I've gone out for a walk, just ask me for the whistle."

If she answered, it must have been too quiet for me to hear, but she heard all right because first in a little while, then again, a second time, a lot later, I heard her say, very, faint "Blow your whistle Mr Levy."

After she asked me that second time and I blew the whistle, my heart was beating in big, slow bubbles, like glue that's just come to the boil. Each bubble filled me up so I couldn't breath and then, as the bubble went down, so the air would come rushing in and rattle down my throat like coals into a cellar, and then, as I finished blowing I don't know what happened. It was just like a firework went off in my head, and then a big blackness, full of soft sinking, and then nothing at all.

How long I stayed like that I don't know. But suddenly I heard Mrs Arnold say very clear, and quite loud, "Blow your whistle, Mr Levy."

And I blew it. And for the first time it whistled properly. It was lovely, and I blew it 'till the cupboard was filled with its screaming and it sounded like guns in my ears - until the firework went off in my head, and there was nothing again. When I woke up everything was very white and light and Bessie was looking down at me. "Hello, Bessie." I said.

She said "Hello Morry."

"I didn't think I should see you so soon, Bessie."

"No," she said. She started to say something more, but didn't speak. Instead she bent down and kissed me, and I could feel on her cheeks why she didn't say any more. "Yes," she said, when she stood up straight again. "They were quick weren't they? Four o'clock they heard the whistle and half-past four you were out."

"Did they get Mrs Arnold out?" I asked.

"Yes," said Bessie. "They got her out at about two o'clock. They'd have got you out then, but I told them I was sure you were working in the front room - I had to go and interfere! But the Doctor says you'll be fine soon, so don't look so worried!"

"Is Mrs Arnold all right,?" I asked.

She was dead already, when they got her out," Bessie said.

A STRIPED SOCK!

Have you ever noticed, that when you look at an old map of the world, there are lots of countries that don't seem to exist anymore? Once upon a time when there were Kingdoms all over the place, although most of them weren't very big. I went on tour with a company of actors playing Shakespeare's plays. We went about from Kingdom to Kingdom, through all sorts of principalities and dominions. And everywhere we went we had a wonderful welcome and all the people came to the theatre to see us play our plays.

But the place I'll never forget was Serenia. – It's no use looking on the map for it now – it's not there any more, now it's just a part of somewhere else and even in those days, before the War, the King must have known that the days of Serenia as a little kingdom were numbered. But even that sad thought didn't stop him from behaving like a proper King and a great gentleman.

He came himself one night to see our play. It was "Henry V", and what polishing of a buckler and brasses there was that night – all the girls practicing their curtsey and the men trying to get their bows right and the producer rushing around saying "For Heaven's sake, do you think you're all going to get knighthoods? The King doesn't want to see you acting off the stage but on it". But as it turned out, he didn't see much of that either.

The play was just getting into its stride – where the Dauphin of France sent young King Henry V a tub of tennis balls and tells him to run away and play, instead of trying to be King of France – and you remember what King Henry says to the messenger in answer? – Well I don't remember it all myself but roughly speaking he thanks the Ambassadors very politely and then says "But I will rise there with so full a glory that I will dazzle all the eyes of France, yea, strike the Dauphin blind to look on us. And tell the pleasant prince this mock of his hath turn'd his balls to gun stones; and his soul shall stand sore-charged for the wasteful vengeance that shall fly with them;"

and that was as far as we got, because the King stood up, and the people in the theatre stood up and we sat there like dummies, as he left the box. There was absolute silence for a bit; and then we tried to carry on, just as the orchestra had re-assembled in the orchestra pit and started to play the National Anthem, so everybody stood up again. Proper chaos it was.

And it wasn't much of a performance either, after all that.

At the end of the show I was sitting in my dressing room feeling pretty miserable. The producer was with me and he was saying, "Well, I must say, they have some very strange ideas of good manners in these parts."

"Oh, I dunno," I said, "I expect he had some jolly good reason, or maybe he just didn't like it."

"Well", said the producer, "he might have waited 'til the end of the act and then gone quietly, you'd have thought that ordinary civil behaviour would ......"

"Look", I said "forget it. I expect the King knows how to behave just as well as you do – he's probably got his reasons."

And as I said it, there was a gentle tap on my door and before I could answer it was opened and the stage-door keeper came in practically bent double, he was a bit fat to get stuck like that and his voice came out like air from a squashed bellows. "Here, is for you to see, something", he said.

"Look chum", I said, "after to-night I've seen everything."

"You know this? She is a small world".

"No, we have not met I think Mr. Slater" said a different voice. And a very dapper man walked into my room. "My name is Struben", he went on, "Count Ignaz Struben. You may go", he said, and the way the doorkeeper went I knew this must be quite somebody around the place. He was in evening clothes with enough orders and medals and ribbons down the front of him for a Favour seller at the boat race.
"May I?" he said, and sat down.

"Oh – yes" I said, "please do, come in. I mean have a cup of tea, there's some in the Thermos, or would you like a ..."

"Mr. Slater", he said, "please do not let me disturb your routine. I am here in the name of

King Boris who has expressed a desire for your company at the Palace this evening. There is a Ball at the Court and the King Graciously extends this invitation to you.

"Well", I said, "actually I haven't got my party dress with me, I don't think...."

"We will stop at you hotel", he said, you may collect whatever is necessary and there will be an apartment at your disposal at the Palace".

And that's what we did. I got my evening clothes and my black patent shoes and a couple of stiff shirts and a couple of pairs of socks – always take two of everything in the theatre, one of anything can always go wrong – a spare collar, all my links and studs. And off we went to the Palace.

It was more like a big house with a few turrets stuck on for luck. But this night it looked very gay, all the windows were shining and music was gusting out of the door and the crowd outside were swaying in waltz-time. There were ooohs and aaahs as we drove up, and a slightly puzzled silence fell as I got out with my bundle of clothes, then somebody said "Artisti" and they all began to clap, and that made me feel better.

Count Ignaz led the way past a flotilla of flunkies up a broad staircase to a beautifully furnished suite of rooms. "The King", he said, "requests that you avail yourself of these his private apartments".

And I felt better still as I unpacked my clothes, unrolled my socks and studded and linked my shirts. By the time I was dressed all I needed was a couple of bits of ribbon and I'd have felt like a king myself. My trousers were a bit short – but a King can wear his trousers how he likes.

Count Struben came back for me and took me down to meet the King. I was announced and the dancing stopped as I walked the whole length of the ballroom to make my bow before him. I felt like a fly on a billiard ball under a strong light. And what was worse as I approached the King I got the feeling that the ladies and gentlemen of the Court were finding something funny about me – hands went up over mouths and ladies giggled quietly behind fans. I knew my trousers were short, but I didn't think they were that bad, and by the time I reached the King I was feeling pretty red around the ears. But he put me completely at ease. I sat at his left, in a chair just below his, and the dancing began again.

The King explained that with the political situation all around his country so tense, he had felt that after that speech about the tennis balls, his visit to the theatre might be given political significance, so he was coming to see "Midsummer Night's Dream" to-morrow, instead. Then he asked me to excuse him for a moment, and after he'd gone the dancing continued and I sat and waited for him.

Feeling jolly uncomfortable too because once the King had gone the sniggering of the dancers began again as they floated past me. I sat there not quite knowing where to put myself. Even when the King came back I didn't feel really comfortable. And then in the end I tried to appear nonchalant – you know, couldn't care less - and I lolled back in my chair and crossed my legs. Well at that a howl of laughter went up – and at last I could see why, I was wearing one plain back sock and one with stripes on. Then quite suddenly the laughter stopped. And I saw that the King was lolling back just like me, with his legs crossed, and just like me he was wearing one black sock and one striped one.

"I hope you don't mind," he said, "I hadn't got a pair like yours, so I borrowed the ones you left in my apartments."

The dancers were the ones who looked red round the ears now –

"I am honoured your majesty", I said.

"Not at all", said the King, "the first duty of a host is the comfort of his guest."

So I've kept that un-matched pair of socks ever since. They're the most regal souvenir I've got.

APPLES A POUND PEARS

It's a long time since I had a barrer, but that's how I started. Fruit and veg piled high, flare lamps when it got dark and pick up and push soon as you saw a copper on the corner – I reckoned that the fines for 'obstruction' would set me back about 25 bob a month on average.

I remember once I'd just been done for the usual, in Bow Street, and I was pushing the barrer out into Covent Garden, to see if I could borrow the fine from a porter pal of mine, when a black saloon came whipping round the corner and nearly had me in the Opera House. It didn't stop and as I opened me mouth to holler I caught a glimpse of the blokes in it. It was Harry Morgan and his mob. A bunch of real big time spivs – so I didn't holler, I kept quiet and started piling the veg back on the barrier.

I'd just about got half the lot all set up again when – wheeee! Round comes another lunatic and over it goes again. This time I really tore off a mouthful, and it wasn't until I'd said some very rude things about his family that I realised it was Inspector Sanderson and his mobile boys from the Station. "We'll go into all that later," he said "– what precisely are you doing here across the middle of the road?"

"Gardening," I said.

"Getting the crop in for Harry Morgan I suppose."

"Harry Morgan – who's he?" If it was a question of keeping on good terms with Harry Morgan or the Police – I chose Harry, after all, the Police don't come after you with pick-axe handles!

"Alright Johnny, we'll get round to you in due course," said the inspector. Get weaving boys.

And off they went. And I started all over again, piling up the goods. It wasn't until I was scooping the last pound or two of apples out of the gutter that I came across a little Gladstone bag tucked in among 'em. As I picked it up it fell open, and I saw wadges of pound notes lying in it like chunks of cabbage in a hippopotamus's mouth.

I knew what must have happened – Harry Morgan had been rumbled doing a pay-roll job and tipped the loot out on to me as he spotted me barrer. He'd be back all right. But then, so would the Police, and I'd already spoilt me chances with them; they wouldn't believe I hadn't been waiting for that bag, even if I handed it over to 'em – and I didn't like to think what Harry Morgan would do if I did that; I felt like a walnut waiting for the crackers to close.

There was only one thing for it – get weaving – and quick, so I shoved off.
I was on home ground round Petticoat Lane and I still hadn't made up me mind what I was going to do, when I passed Tony Caserto's Ice Cream shop – I didn't so much see it as hear it - Tony always provides his own music while he works. Ta ra ra ra Tara.

And that gave me an idea. I went in. Tony's wife was serving.

"Ullo Giovani – Wharrer you wan' – Chocolate, Vanilla, Strawberry or Pistachio?"

"I wan' Tony," I said.

" `E's a down stair mixing."

"I know," I said, "it's a wonder he don't sour the cream!"

"You go down and shurrimup." The singing got louder and I got nearer.

"Ta Ra Ra Ra Ra R-Ra. Ullo Johnny boy Ta Ra Ra "

"Tony.."

"Ra Ra-Ra"

"Tony – I need some help"

"Hey? You want me to teach you to sing eh? we make an aria: Apples a pound a Pearers."

"Not today."

"You like my singing? "

"Only when it stops."

"When it. Oh ho is a witty feller. What can I do to you."

"You still got that car Tony?"

"Yes."

Good

"But I couldn't lend it to you – is a death trap."

"But Tony ...."

"Is no brakes"

"Tony I don't......"

"The radiator leaks like a colander"

"Listen Tony ..."

"The steering wheel come off in my hands last week – I tell you it's a a......"

"Tony I want to buy it!"

"........ wonderful car, it skims along as smooth as cream – my cream – is as quiet as a fish in the sea. It is a ....."

"Death trap – I know."

"Oh stupido – I joke."

"Yes – how much is the joke worth?"
"£250. ..... All right special for you a reduction, £100."

"Tony," I said, "you got noughts before the eyes
– I'll give you £50."

We settled for £60., and while he went to get
the car from the garage, I dug the money out
of the bag.

"Wharappened to you Johnny," he said, when he
get back, "you come into money or something?"

"Tony," I said, "you haven't seen me for months,
I never had any money and you never had a car
– get it."

"Yeh – I get it – Johnny you done nothing
crocked?"

"Look Tony, if the road bends you gotta go with
it. I haven't done anything, but the less you
know about what I haven't done, the better it'll
be for you."

"O.K. Johnny, if I'd seen you I'd have wished
you good luck with the car if I'd sold you a car,
but I didn't so I won't......."

"That's right Tony," I said, "you've got it, so long."

I got out of London sharpish, without anyone I knew seeing me and after I'd been rolling for about twenty miles I began to breathe more often. I kept to the back doubles most of the way, and I'd got myself well and truly lost, when the car began to let off steam – sounded like a soda siphon when all you get is gas – the rad was as dry as a magistrate's eye – Tony was right, it leaked. Well there was nothing for it but to bash on slowly until I saw somewhere I could fill up, though what with the steam and headlights that were so dipped they were practically submerged, there wasn't much hope of seeing anything. Still, I plugged along, getting further into the country, with the car rattling like a chain factory, until suddenly a bright flash of light flicked across the road a couple of times and the second time I spotted a little pig standing in its beam. I slammed on the footbrake, but that needed about 50 yards to work in – I'd had the handbrake on since I left London – Tony was right, it didn't work. So I wrenched the steering over, but it didn't do any good either: there was a bump and a horrid – weeeeek!!!

The light flooded across the road again as the swing door of a four ale bar was punched open and there lay the pig quiet and still in the yellow beam.

"Ah" – said a bloke in the doorway - "I could drive better with me eyes closed!"

"Go on," I said, "have a try." And I gave him the steering wheel – Tony was right, it came off.

I picked the pig up in my arms and the blokes in the doorway dropped back to let me through. Nobody spoke, except the wireless, and as I walked into the bar the nine o'clock gentleman was saying, "And the Minister assured the Meeting that the bacon ration would be maintained so long as there was enough bacon."

"Well," I said, putting the pig on the bar, this should help, ha ha ha ha." I reckon the pig thought it was funnier than they did. And there was a deadly hush as the Newsman said:

"And now here is a police message: This afternoon three armed men held up and robbed a Bank messenger in Cambridge Circus. Three men questioned subsequently have been released and the police are anxious to interview ...."

I reached over and switched it off – "Can't hear yourself give an order with that on can you?" – I knew who the police wanted to interview – same bloke that Harry Morgan and his boys were looking for – me.

Now – who's ready for a pint, I said. Nobody said anything, though there was a wet gleam in one or two eyes – particularly one old geezer, his were practically dribbling. "Come on Dad," I said, "what'll it be?"

"Five pounds."

"Five pounds? – how d'you want it – pint glass full of small silver – What are you talking about, £5.?"

"For my pig."

"What do you feed him on gold dust – he's only a half-pint pig anyway."

"Special kind of pig, stays small."

"Well, can I help it if your pig comes rolling out of a pub drunk and incapable?"

The Landlord leant across the bar – "I'll have you know that no dumb animal is served with intoxicating liquor in this house."

I looked round the bar – they all stood there looking at me. I see what you mean, I said. I peeled five one-ers off the wad I'd put in my pocket and gave them to the old boy. After that it was like I'd pulled the stopper out of a bottle – the whole room started gurgling at once.

"Pint o' mixed please George"

"Pint o' rough George"

"One from the wood George"

"I'll 'ave an ale – I'll 'ave a bitter".

If I'd come by canoe I could have paddled all the way back to London in the beer I bought. I couldn't help liking the way they all stood by each other. You know, they wanted to see justice done before they'd have a drink with me. It was that, I think, that made me make up my mind to stay in the village – I never knew when I might need somebody to stand by me – Although I must say the ancient bargainer didn't exactly fall over himself with joy when I said I though of living in those parts for a while.

"Is there a hotel I could put up in?"

"Ahh..... No."

"Anybody take lodgers?"

"Ahh..... No."

"Well has anybody got a spreading chestnut tree and a couple of blankets!"

"Well there's me mum's old cottage." I looked across the room. The bloke talking was the only one without a pint in his hand – sitting over in the corner.

"Well what about your Mum?" I said.

"She don't live there."

"Where does she live then?"

"With me Dad."

There was a lot more conversation like that, before I found out that he used the cottage and it was sort of furnished. It would cost me 3 quid a week. His name was Nathaniel, and he could go and live with Dad an' all.

We made a deal of it and I said "Come on Nat have a drink on it"

"Nat ain't drinking,"

"I can see that George," I said "that's why I'm offering him one."

"Can I have one George, just a little one?"

"Now Nat, you've had one and to-morrow's Saturday."

"I know George, but I feel fine," said Nat: He stood up – and fell flat on his face.

"Ah," said George, "can't take liquor, and he's our fast bowler see – we have to keep him tidy for Saturday afternoon, his head's all right, but he's got legs like a card table."

"Well," I said, "put him in the car and we'll have a look at this cottage – oh and can I have some water for the radiator?"

"Sorry," He said – "we're short on water, will a couple of pints of ale do?" It did it. But I don't know what it did to the car; what with Nathaniel and his folding legs, a slab of cold pork, no brakes, no lights, no steering and the engine going Grrr – hic – Grrr – hic – Grrr – that was quite a journey. Sobered Nathaniel up anyway.

I couldn't see much of the cottage when we got there, it was the usual one up and one down and the rest out back. The furniture was mostly empty packing cases – well it was something to sit on so long as you didn't mind the splinters. There was paraffin for lighting and cooking and the bed was an old four poster that had caved in, so it looked like a four cornered roundabout waiting for the music to start.

Nat showed me where he kept things and told me there was poultry out back and a T.B. tested cow in the barn, so I could have eggs and milk at a price to be fixed with Dad.

I didn't argue the toss – I was so flaked out, all I wanted to do was to get me head down. So he went and I got me little black bag and me little white pig and up I went and plonked 'em on the chest of draws – I'd paid £5 for the corpse and if I couldn't sell it I was going to live off it, so I didn't want to leave it lying around. I fell into the bed – it was about a two foot drop – the mattress wasn't in the frame it was on the floor – and I went out like a light.

I didn't seem to have been sleeping for more than about five minutes when I woke up with a cold sweat prickling out all over me. Something was moving in the room – I could hear a kind of strangled breathing – I nearly suffocated trying not to. I lifted my head very slowly, like a blown tulip in fresh water, until I could see over the edge of the frame of the bed – I looked towards the sound and I saw a pale luminous shape about four foot high, and as I looked it seemed to launch itself slowly through the air towards me – I closed my eyes. There was a dull thud by the side of the bed – I could almost feel the breathing now – hot on my face – I kept my eyes tight shut – "who are you?" I said.

Chworp – chworp – chworp, came the answer.

I opened my eyes – It was the pig – and there was I with dawn breaking through the window and my breakfast looking at me over the edge of the bed.

In daylight the cottage looked like a design for a bomb-damage claim. The first thing I did was to check up on the little black bag that Harry Morgan had knocked off from the Bank Messenger and dumped in my barrer when the cops got too hot. With the money I spent on buying Tony Caserto's car, drinks in the pub, the price of the pig and a month's rent in advance, I reckoned that there must've been about 480 quid that the Police and Harry Morgan wanted to see me about.

Well the thing to do, I decided, was to use the money to invest in local industry that would show me a quick turn-over – I didn't mind if it turned a little sour – so long as it turned quick. Then when the numbers were up to 480 again – or a round 500 for luck, I'd see the police got the bag, with a strictly anonymous note, and then lie low 'till Morgan got done for some other job – which was bound to happen pretty soon.

By the time I'd thought all that out I was pretty hungry. Nathaniel had left me a slice of bacon, so I put it on the paraffin cooker to do slowly while I went out the back to wash. It was a fine bright morning and the sun had got the earth cooking gently; it smelt like a meal fit for a lord. Hummph – Haah – this is the life. I grabbed the pump handle and started working it up and down, and shoved me head underneath – nothing happened for a bit, then the nozzle fell off and hit me in the back of the neck and as I came up rubbing my head the water came out of the hole in the top and slapped me in the face.

I screwed the nozzle on again and filled a kettle for a cuppa, the bacon was just catching jaundice at the edges, then I remembered what Nathaniel said about poultry and the T.B. tested cow – So I took my cup and I went out to the barn – one cup in the morning is usually enough for me and there's no sense in being greedy – There was the cow, don't they look fierce? – I'm glad I never tried to milk a bull – and there was all the apparatus – all I had to do was pull, but I didn't know which one to pull – so I picked the middle one and held me cup underneath. Mmmmdoah, said the cow – and scared me witless. I dropped the cup and she trod on it – well I've had tea without milk before, I thought, and at least a lemon doesn't answer back when you squeeze it.

Before I returned to the house, I thought I'd have a look around for the poultry, we used to keep chickens in the back yard, so I knew how to handle them. I scouted around the half acre but I couldn't find a feather. Then just by a brook that was talking its head off at the bottom of the land, I spotted a big rough and ready sort of nest on the ground with a smashing big egg in it. I picked it up and stuck it in my pocket – and I was just thinking that if I could get 50 or 60 hens that laid that kind of egg I'd be on my way to getting that Bank money back, when I heard a noise like a welding burner behind me – it was a blooming great goose. It came in swinging with both wings and caught me under the ribs with a left hook that had me clean into the drink. It followed me in and got me in the seat of the pants with a nice straight neck that shot me into the bank again and then chased me all the way back to the house. The pig was standing by the paraffin cooker as I slammed the back door.

Oh – I said – nice of you to come down for your breakfast. Then I smelt me breakfast it was all going up in a cloud of blue smoke from the frying pan – I grabbed the pan and didn't realise how hot it was until I saw blue smoke going up from my hand as well – I fished in my pocket for a hanky and brought out a handful of scrambled egg – goose-egg, uncooked.

Chorp – chorp – chorp-chorp went the pig. "Funny eh?" I said, "all right chum I'll deal with you first."

So I got a bit of string around his neck, and the pair of us went off down the village street. Funny, he didn't seem to mind at all, didn't pull or struggle or anything, just walked to heel like a bald sheep dog. He was so quiet I didn't notice I'd lost him until some kids started laughing at me holding on to an empty bit of string – and d'you know I almost felt glad, I could never even take the dog to a vet, me Dad always had to do it for me. I was close to the Butcher's shop though, so I popped in to see if there was any offal going, and there was the pig standing on the counter. "Living dangerously aren't you?" I said.

"Ah, often come in here does Percy," said the Butcher bloke patting him on the back.

"What – once a week for a close shave I s'pose? Well this time he's had it – he's come to be pickled."

"Pickled?"

"Yes, I love him so much I'm going to eat him. Four times a day if necessary."

"Ah – Ministry won't let you do any private slaughtering."

"This ain't slaughtering, it's self defence."

We argued up and down, but the only help he gave me was the name of a Farmer who'd come to the district lately and nobody liked anyway. I didn't like him much meself - His name was Harrigan. He was a heavy surly bloke with still black eyes like wet cobble-stones.

"No" – he said – "we only slaughter under Licence."

"Pity," I said, "might have been able to put you in the way of a bit of trade."

I saw the thought splash through his eyes. "Trade?"

"Yes, you know, one or two big people I know in London who get a bit short."

He looked at me. "I'll be in the sheds on Tuesday – bring your pig up Tuesday night before I clean up."

That was all, then he shut the door in my face. Still it wasn't his manners I needed, it was his pork – I knew there was a racket in pork, and if I could get in on it, I'd have that money back to the police in no time.

So the next Tuesday night, round about half past nine I got Percy into a sack – I wasn't taking no more chances with bits of string – and I walked out of the cottage slap into the arms of a policeman. He was the first copper I'd seen since I left London – I nearly curdled.

"What you got in that sack?"

"Meat" – I said.

He took it from me and Percy jumped out. "Bit fresh ain't it – Put him back."

"You let 'im out – you put 'im back," I said.
It took him and his two mates from the police car parked in the lane 35 minutes to get Percy back into the sack.

Then they took the pair of us off to the Cop-shop in the big village about 4 miles up the road.

"What's this all in aid of?" I said when we got there.

"I s'pose you didn't know Farmer Harrigan has lost a pig?"

"No," I said.

"And of course that wouldn't be his pig?" said the sergeant pointing at the sack.

"That's right," I said, it wouldn't – "let him out and I'll prove it."

Percy came out like a Duchess in a dudgeon – ever bristle on his body was standing up with rage.

"There's a good Percy – what 'ey do?" Come to Daddy.

The copper looked at me – so did Percy – Chorp Chorp Chorp, he said – he was livid. He backed away across the table and before we knew what he was up to, he made a bunk for it – out of the window. There was a WHEEEK and a crash.

We all rushed to the window. There was a girl and a bicycle and Percy, all tangled up like a basket of knitting, in the middle of the road.

"Why can't you keep your pig under control?" – she said to me.

"His pig?" – said the copper.

"Of course – he bought it from old Rumbold when he ran over it."

So we ended up all going back together – her pedalling, me on the step and Percy trotting alongside and as we got to the village a big van came tearing out of the lane leading to Harrigan's place and went whizzing off in front of us.

"That was Harrigan wasn't it?" I said.

"Yes, we call that his Black Market Van."

"Black Market?"

Yes, Police reckon he's all tied up in it, but they ain't caught 'im at it yet.
No of course they hadn't and wouldn't either so long as he could find a clot like me to keep 'em occupied while he got on with it.. I might be able to put you in the way of a bit of trade ......

oh very clever – he must be laughing his head off.

Mark you, that was only the start of my efforts to make a fast buck

For instance I was in a pub when a couple of blokes did a deal over a game of darts for a treeful of walnuts – it was weird to watch 'em.

"Middle for diddle."
50
"You're off"
Double top
"5 made – 35 to muck."
"Right its yours."
"Done."

Well, that meant one of 'em had bought the crop for 35 nicker. I checked up and I found the average bearing for this bloke's trees was 400 - 600 pounds – well, work it out for yourselves. Three and six a pound they go on the barrer – I could be an honest man again in no time at that rate. So I got myself a tree full for 48 quid – Yes £48, I was a bit unlucky, I went out on treble 16's. But anyway it still smelt like a good profit – "when can I come up for 'em?" I said.

"Well you can come and have a look at the tree this afternoon."

So I go up there and he shows me a tree that looks like an aged bride with stale confetti in her hair.

"Where's the nuts?" I said.

"They'll be there boy, in October."

"October?!"

So there I was with 48 quids worth of green pea-nuts and old lace, and if it didn't get too hot or too cold, or rain too much or too little, I might see my money in 5 months' time.

Then there was the cricket match – I'm not really proud of this, but I was getting desperate. You remember I told you I saw Nathaniel the fast bowler fall flat on his face after one pint – well, I bet 50 quid against the local side and filled Nathaniel full of beer – 11 pints each we had on a Saturday morning. I got meself into a deck chair and didn't wake up until the match was over. I found the Bookie in the pub.

"Well, I said, when do I get paid?"

"Get paid," he said – "we won lad, and the skipper says I was to give you a vote of thanks for filling our Nat up with beer."

"Thanks – Look with me own eyes I saw him cave in like a house of cards on one pint."

"Ah no – that were rough cider."

Well you can't cope with that sort of thing can you – So on the Sunday I decided to pack up. It was a day like Heaven had a headache – the air was frightened to breathe and the sky was ready to burst out crying if anyone looked at it. Well I smartened meself up, put on my pointed patents and went for a last stroll through the village to show 'em I didn't care – but it was funny, there was nobody there to care whether I cared or not, the place was empty. I got to the pub bang on opening time, just as George was closing it.

"Oy George, you ought to be taking that padlock off not putting it on," I said.

"No sense in opening, everybody's in Farmer Everton's fields picking."

"Picking what?"

"Strawberries – and I'm on my way to join 'em." And off he went with me tagging along behind.

"What's the panic?" I said.

"Air Ministry warning. Heavy thunderstorms in this area – whole early crop will be ruined if we don't get it in."

Farmer Everton's looked like a scene out of Uncle Tom's Cabin – the whole village double inching their way through the strawberry beds, the back of their shirts and blouses and dresses turning as black as the sky, and the sweat running down off the ends of their noses and finger tips. I tell you it made me hot to look at them. I was just going to move off and mind me own business when the girl who'd pedalled me home the night I was pinched stood up in front of me and said – "Oh hallo come to give us a hand? – that's nice." She mopped her face with her arm, but as her arm was as wet as her face it didn't make much difference – "No love," I said, "it's not my day for a Turkish bath."

"Oh," she said.

"Sorry," I said.

"That's alright," she said, "I should have known better."

Well – when I found somewhere to put me coat, I got stuck in alongside her – she gave me a look and then she smiled at me, and when I looked round they were all smiling at me – not that there was much time for smiling - but for the first time I felt that I was with 'em on the inside. Mark you, I'll tell you one thing - never go picking in pointed patents - after about half an hour they were as cracked as sealing wax on a Christmas parcel. I suppose we'd got about three quarters of the crop in when the lightning unzipped the sky and let the water out. So we left the other quarter and steamed off into the big packing shed.

Farmer Everton was nearly dancing with joy. It would all be sold on a profit sharing basis, he said.

Funny ain't it - the one thing that never occurred to me was that I might get that stolen money back by working for it. And we listened while Everton phoned his Agents.

"Hullo Herbert - Yes, that's right, we've got the storm - Listen (and held up the receiver so Herbert could hear the rain playing the big drum on the roof) No, No - everything's all right - we got it in - well three quarters of it. When can you take it. What - But it'll be ruined. Yes - yes - I see."

He had the same kind of conversation with three other people and then he came and told us, that nobody had any transport free to pick up the crop they'd planned to collect at the end of the week, and anyway they weren't ready to market the stuff yet.

"Not ready!" I said, look you get it to London – I'll show you how to market it." They looked at me – "come on," I said, "London – by dawn."

And you should have seen the copper's face when the convoy hit Lambeth Bridge as the sun came up – class cars, fast cars, the village hearse – a tractor towing a string of carts and pony traps – anything that could roll. Then I whipped round the offices and hired, begged and borrowed every barrer I could lay me hands on. We got 'em loaded and out they went trickling through the streets of London, like rain on a window. I whizzed round on a bike showing 'em how to shout, how to push, how to keep out of trouble with the traffic and the police and the other barrow boys and I even found time to drop a load into Tony Caserto's Ice cream shop.

"Hey Johnny, Grazie – I make you the best strawberry sundae you ever had on a Thursday." "Sorry Tony, no time – Has Harry Morgan gone inside yet?"

"No, and he's looking for you."

"I Know – well let me know when he takes a trip – the name of the village is on the wrapping paper over the strawberries."

"O.K. Johnny – grazie – good luck."

Well, - it was a sell out. We got back to the village and shared out in the pub and by the time we finished there was nearly enough in my little black bag to send back to the police. Farmer Everton was buying pints right, left and centre when suddenly I heard outside in the street – "Apples a Pound Pears – Johnny where are you. Apples a p------"

"Tony," I shouted – "in here." He came darting into the pub.

"Johnny – Harry Morgan, he's coming – he heard you was a selling strawberries and he find a wrapping paper."

Everybody was quiet, listening. "Well - so long all, I said, I've got to run." I grabbed me bag.

Chwoop, Chwoop, Chwoop, went Percy the pig. "Sorry Percy," I said, "can't take you. Joe – you can have him back with my love."

"Ah ta" – said Joe and he cocked his head at the sound of a car approaching, then flicked open the swing door and pushed poor old Percy out just as the car came roaring up.

"Joe," I shouted.

Wheeeeek – went Percy.

Crash – went the car.

Then nothing at all, except a nightingale.

We all moved to the door and in the beam of light as it opened I saw Harry Morgan looking down at poor pale Percy in the middle of the road.

He looked up.

"Hello Johnny," he said.

"Hm, hm," I said.
"And Tony too eh? my old friend Tony."

"No – is a some other Tony you know – not me." Tony backed away into the pub and let the door swing to – it swung slap on to the little black bag that was under my arm – out went the bag like an orange pip, straight to Harry Morgan.

"Thanks," he said, and he went.

Tony and me watched him go sitting on the step on the pub. Joe picked up poor Percy and came and joined us. Before we could say anything there was a terrific crash up the road as Farmer Harrigan's van came out of his lane with a police car on his tail, slap into Morgan's car and the road was covered with black market pork and red faced gents with the copper picking up more villains in five minutes than they'd seen in these parts since Dick Turpin's ride.

"About time they caught up with Harrigan" – said old Joe – "this'll be a good night for them."

"Yes," I said, "a good night for everybody except me – oh and you – I'm sorry about Percy."

"Oh that's all right he's used to it" – he slapped Percy on the back – "wake up, you can stop pretending." Percy opened one eye and looked at me – Chworp – he said, and almost seemed to grin.

BYE BYE GERTY

I met Fred the other day; first time for a couple of years. He was just getting out of a smashing new lorry – streamlined like the Royal Scot and when he shut the door it sounded like velvet cushions.

"Going up in the world eh?" I said, "what happened to your old bus?"

"Oh," he said, "I got rid of Gerty some time ago. Bits falling off her all over the place. Remember when you drove in her the driver's door used to fall open every time you took a left hand bend?"

"That's right," I said, "and the driving mirror used to swing round with it, and end up back to front on the windscreen so's you couldn't see where you were going – yeah, I remember."

"That's right," said Fred. "Well I had to get rid of her poor old girl. The last straw came some time back when I was taking a night load of jigs and tools across the moors. Dirty night it was, the wind bagpiping through the gorse and I got right out into the open spaces about three in the morning. I felt as lonely as a fly in a fridge. And you know when you're like that you begin thinking things – and I couldn't help thinking of the report in the evening papers about the feller who'd ducked out of Broadmoor while everybody was at lunch. Nasty character he sounded by all accounts. With a couple of murders to his credit. Well, I was driving along, as I say, not feeling too chipper about it all, when I noticed that I wasn't getting a really clear line on the road ahead – the crown of the road wasn't showing up in the offside head-light at all – it was just getting a yellow edge from the near-side lamp. I dipped up and down a couple of times and tried switching on and off, but it was no good. The offside head-light was out good and proper. I couldn't drive right across the moor like that, so there was nothing for it but to get out and fix it.

It was like stepping off the bridge of a ship straight into the North Atlantic. The wind whistled and sliced at me as stood in from of the radiator and gave the lamp a bash, usually works that, giving the lamp a bash, if there's a faulty connection. Didn't this time – there was a crash that disappeared into the howling wind and I was still standing there alone half in the dark, in the middle of the moors. Proper queasy I was beginning to feel. I took another slug at the lamp, a bit panicky I was this time, but this time it worked the light came on. That made me feel a bit better. A bit better until I looked up, and there behind the lamp reflected in the light that was bouncing back off me, I saw a face. A face watching me. The hairs on the back of my neck stood out like tuning forks in the wind. Hullo, I said, but he didn't answer, just stayed there watching, a hideous face it was with gleaming eyes. I tell you, I reckoned I'd had my lot, but I wasn't going to let him have it all his own way. I moved round very gently from the headlight, out of the corner of my eye I watched him watching me. I bent over the bonnet and fiddled with the catches, like I was going to check something in the engine. I kept my left shoulder down so he couldn't see my right fist curling ready to hook into him. As I bent over I grinned at him all friendly like. He grinned back, a horrible sight it was, white skin stretched tight round fangy teeth. And at that moment I brought up my right – and smashed full into the face.. and nearly bust my wrist on the driving mirror –

- 208 -

the door had swung open when I hit the headlamp and all I'd been seeing was me! Well I had to get rid of Gerty after that.

COME ON STEVE!

"Who flogged the bacon?" croaked the corporal in the opposite bed. He croaked because they'd removed his tonsils and left him with a croak instead! And somebody had told him that there, in the Reserve Hospital in Rome, in 1945, we were supposed to get army rations. Trouble was, that while he was under the anaesthetic, he had dreamt that army rations included bacon!

Anyway, that's lousy way of being woken out of a gentle sleep. It was about 7.30 a.m. The day shone brightly through the tall, pointed windows which made the whole place feel like the inside of a church. You always felt that any minute now Bing Crosby would come floating down the ward, on pink wings, singing Ave Maria.

Old Steve was already buzzing around in his wheelchair, carrying cups of tea and bread with a promise of butter on it but not much more, from bed to bed, to help the high-heeled Italian number. He did it just for the Hell of it and the joy of living, though you wouldn't think that there could be much joy in living for a Jockey who'd lost a leg when his horse fell on him. But Steve had been out of his bed, and tucking himself into his chair, long before I was carefully wiping the soap out of my eyes, so as not to disturb any of the sleep; and I expect that by now he had tidied up the library, emptied the ash-trays, collected yesterday's newspapers and anything else he could think of.

I had sort of sensed him buzzing around, being useful, through my dozing and I had a dim feeling that this morning he was being especially useful. And I knew the reason – but couldn't place it.

And I didn't really have much time to think about it during the morning. Steve came and asked me if there was anything I wanted him to bring in, so I gave him my empty and asked him to see if the bar would fill it and trust me until the Pay Corps remembered me. He'd been doing that sort of thing for me ever since I came in three weeks before.

I remember the first time I saw Steve: a round, toothless face, like a stored apple that's shrunk a bit inside its skin. Just for a second it was, through the ether haze. Then my leg came alive again and I passed out.

From then on he'd made a point of seeing that I had everything he could put my way – vino from the bar, the extra spoonful of Nestles – you know, whatever was going, and all he wanted back was that I should be friendly and chat a little.

We chatted enough for me to find out quite a lot about him. How, as a kid he'd been sent away from London by a charity, to get over pneumonia, and how he found that he liked animals, so cleared out of home and got taken on by a racing stables at Epson, after he'd landed there with a gypsy outfit.

It took quite a while to sort it all out, but it went something like this: he went to the fair up on Hampstead and spent most of the time playing houses and Red-Indians and other funny games with a gypsy girl of his own age; but with gypsies, his own age – about fourteen or so – was quite a lot of years to have behind you, so by the time he had stopped with the outfit long enough for it to reach Epsom, Papa Gypsy was getting curious about just how honourable his middle-aged intentions were. He was so curious that he scared Steve into a horse box that happened to be around and Steve didn't come out until the box arrived back at its stables. At which time the boss said that anyone who could stay that close to a race horse, for that long, and not get trampled to death, must be good with horses, so he gave him a job!

As far as I can make out he did all right. He stayed small and got to be a jockey – but never really the tops – maybe because there was another Steve around at the same time who got all the shouting, and I think it was that which, in the end, made him pack up and leave the country. It's the same with all those professions that get the public cheering for you and asking you to sign books or balls or their shirts – it's the yelling that tells you you're on top that gets to you, until you can't be happy anywhere except on top and that yell means more to you than money, or home, and you'll go anywhere to get it.

And Steve went everywhere: South America, North America, Paris, Berlin, all over Europe, ending up in Rome, which was where he had been riding nine months earlier, when he crashed. When he came round he was in the British Reserve Hospital, with a right leg that hurt like

Hell – although he wasn't wearing it any more – and he nearly died when he found out.

He'd been way out in front and at the last fence when his horse landed in his lap and he could still hear the crowd yelling "Come on Steve". The whole crowd were at it, even if they were losing while he was winning. He was a popular little bloke and they were glad for him to win. And "Come on Steve" is a good shout to hear – even if it has got an Italian accent,

So you see, after all those months of healing all he could remember was that yell as he was winning. It was like he'd never lost a race; never had that bad patch, when no-one would hire him. No, all he could remember was that he was winning and all the other times that he had won and the crowd had shouted "Come on Steve".

Anyway, that morning I'd been writing letters and the doctors had been looking and pulling and pushing and generally mucking me about, so I hadn't thought any more about what was special about it for Steve, and even when he came steaming in like rain in Burma, with my empty bottle still stuck down by the arm of his chair and never a grape in sight, I still didn't cotton on.

In fact, it wasn't until a plump little signor fussed up through the ward, carrying a long, brown paper parcel and the screens went round Steve's bed that anything clicked at all, and then, when I thought of that grin and the red that spread all the way from his neck to his hairline – which started some three inches back from his forehead – I remembered what it was that the tubby gent was handing him, like first prize for a good boy. It was Steve's new leg.

Soon they came out from behind the screens. Steve was upright but leaning heavily on the little Italian on one side and his stick on the other. They did a couple of paces like Siamese twins trying out a new dance step. Steve was sweating and you could see he hurt.

The ward was quiet. Not like the usual hospital quiet but quiet like a cup final crowd before a penalty kick. The corp. stopped croaking, the kid with the earache, in the next bed to me, stopped grizzling for his mum and the nurse with the first trolley-load of lunches stopped in the doorway and watched.

Steve let go of his escort and stood stock still for a second, taking his weight and getting his balance, and we all took that first pace with him; we all felt sick in our stomachs as he

- 215 -

lurched and would have gone flat on his face but for the little man.

"No use," gasped Steve, "I can't". He didn't say it, it just came out on his breath, but we heard every word in the stillness.

"Try, amigo, try." Said the leg man.

"No," said Steve, "it's a wash out." But the Italian straightened him out again and Steve held his hand and took one step, and then another. Then he let go and stood alone, swaying a bit. "Come on Steve," I whispered. He heard me and the veins stood out purple across his bald head as he tried. I said it again "Come on Steve!" and suddenly the leg moved forward and the other leg came up to it and then the whole ward cut loose. "Come on Steve!" they yelled. "Come on Steve!"

And he stepped again and again and again, and we could see that he was laughing fit to crack his face in half. We could see that, as he laughed, tears were running down his face into his gummy mouth. And from Via Savour to Corso Huberto you could hear us shouting – "Come on Steve!"

FIRST LOVE.

She stood a bit high off the ground did Mabel, a bit high and a bit square. She wasn't really very good looking and somehow she always had an air of wearing glasses. But she was my first car and we all loved her. Specially my boy Michael.

I'll never forget the look on his face when I drove her up to the shop for the first time. It was love at first sight. He walked all round her without saying a word, but you could see that for him she was beautiful, from her polished brass work to the yellow painted spokes in her wheels. When he got to the number plate he read it out in a hushed voice M A B E. 1 – Mabel. And Mabel she stayed, though I never found out how she got a number like that.

She became one of the family; she shared all our joys and sorrows. Particularly the worse sorrow of all when I had to sell her. Things hadn't bee going too well with the business – some bills had to be met and Mabel was the only way I could find of meeting them, so she had to go.

I got up at half past five one winter's morning and sneaked out of the bedroom down through the shop and out into the yard. There she stood. Sad in the rain. Patient, willing, trusting. One turn of the handle and she barked into life, like an old dog I was taking to the vet for the last time. She knew it was the last time, but she didn't make a fuss. I tell you straight there was more than rain in my eyes as I drove her out of the yard.

When I got home for breakfast, the place was in an uproar, Michael had gone. His bed hadn't been slept in and nobody'd seen him since he'd said goodnight at half past nine the night before. They'd 'phoned his grandma, his favourite Aunty and his best pal from school – but nobody'd seen hair not hide of him.

I got the sergeant in from the police station up the road and He'd just about got all the particulars when Mabel drew up outside the shop.

Here, said the bloke I'd sold her to, you left something in the car. And out got Michael.

He was in the luggage boot, the feller said, I thought you might need him, I've got one anyway.

His laugh was lost in the grinding of Mabel's gears and we all stood on the pavement and watched her drive away. Michael's hand was in mine – Then "Come on" said his mother, "you've caused enough trouble without getting us all pneumonia." As she went into the shop she wiped her face on her apron – and pretended it was rain.

Michael was crying as we followed up the back stairs to the kitchen. "Now stop it boy" I said, "you'll be getting your mother all upset. Anyway things'll get better and we'll have another car one day."

"But I don't want another car dad," he said, "I want that one, I want Mabel."

Well that's water under the bridge now. When Mabel drove out of my life that day, she seemed to take all my troubles with her. I cleaned up my debts. Things began to go better at the shop, and it wasn't very long before I had two shops, then three, and when I'd got a few more I bought my way into a Chain Store group and from then on I was in business in a big way, and I have been ever since.

Of course it wasn't long before I got that car like I told Michael I would. But he was never very interested in it, nor was he interested in any of the others we'd had by the time he was coming up for his eighteenth birthday. I spoke to him about it one day. "What d'you want for your birthday Mike?" I asked him.

Oh I don't know dad, he said, there's not much I want really.

Nice way to be son, I said.

All the same, I knew what he was going to get for his birthday. It was the present I'd been waiting to give him ever since I broke his heart eleven years before. I was going to give him a car. A car to take to University with him. A car that was going to make anything else in Oxford look like a tin lizzie.

I'd been to the Motor Show, and I'd ordered the best - nothing flashy – Mike was like that, but the best. And everything there was to go with it. About fifteen hundred pounds it set me back – and mark you I'm talking of days when a pound wasn't just a word on a weighing machine.

Well, Mike's eighteenth birthday arrived. It was a wet day, but I was as excited as a June bride. I'd had the car driven round to the front of the house. It stood there gleaming in the rain, everything that power and dignity and money could make it. I went back into the house and waited for Michael in the breakfast room. When he didn't come down by half past nine, I sent somebody to look for him. He wasn't in the house, nobody'd seen him since dinner the night before.

Of course, this time there wasn't any question of going for the policeman up the road – but it was worrying – disappointing too, on his birthday. I was still hanging about at half hat ten hoping I'd see him before I had to leave the house, when he came in from the direction from the stables.

"Gosh I'm hungry," he said.

"Well you're late for breakfast," I said, "but I expect they'll find you some as it's your birthday – Many happy returns."

"Oh, thanks dad," he said.

"But before you start eating I've got something to show you," I said, "come on."

We went out the front. For a moment Michael didn't speak, then, "Gosh dad" he said, "is that mine!"
"All yours son," I said.

"Gosh!" He said again, "but dad you shouldn't have done it."

"Why not boy?" I said, "I want you to have the best."

"No dad, I don't mean that," he said, "you see I've already bought myself my present from you."

"Oh you have," I said, "well, that's nice for me. What have I brought you?"

"It's in the stable," he said.

"Don't tell me you've brought a horse," I said.

"Well dad," he said "... I ... come and look."

I went out and there in the stable yard I looked at what Michael had bought.
There she stood, high in the front and a bit square – Looking now as if she needed glasses – M.A.B.E.1. MABEL. – and there was more than rain in my eyes.

IF THE CAP FITS

When you walk into my house, one of the first things you see is a helmet on a wig stand. Strange? Well, I keep it as a reminder of the dear dead days beyond recall.

People are always asking – how do you go on the stage? how do you learn? is it better to go to a school, or go into a repertory company? – and do you do either, or both and in any case why can't you start at the top?

Well, last things first. If you start at the top there's nowhere left to go but down, and it's always much more fun going up. A famous actor once said that success on the stage is 98 per cent luck, and two per cent talent. Well, I wouldn't go all the way with him, but he's certainly got something there.

Years ago, long before the War, when I was working as a commercial traveller, selling dog-biscuits and bicycles and paper doilies and cake-decorations, I used to spend all my spare time acting and producing plays with some very good amateur companies – and we did lots of good things too – Gilbert & Sullivan and Shaw and Shakespeare. And I'd probably have stayed that way if a very good actor called Michael Ransom, whom I'd always admired, hadn't come to one of our shows; and congratulated me on my performance afterwards.

Poor chap, he didn't know what he was letting himself in for. The very next chance I had I called at his stage door and he saw me and said "don't" – I must have seen him about a dozen times over the next week or so and every time he said "don't" – don't go on the stage – if you've got a good job keep it, and enjoy theatre as a hobby; as a life, it's heartbreaking and as a living it's hopeless. It's like a slot machine, he said, a slot machine, you put your hopes into it and even if anything comes out, it's never the prize you wanted.

Well, I couldn't have had fairer warning than that could I – but I thought I knew better.

I wasn't so sure about it a few weeks later though, when I'd given up my job and spent my savings.

Then one evening I read that Michael Ransom was working at Denwood Studios on a big new production of "Julius Caesar" – Well I thought, he'll probably call me all kinds of a fool, but perhaps he could help me get a part in the picture.

So, next day I hitch-hiked down to Denwood – it was clean collar or a bus. So I hitch-hiked – got my new collar a bit shop-soiled in the back of a cement lorry, but I still felt smart and that's always important.

The man on the Gate looked like an Admiral, but he didn't have a blind eye. I tried to saunter through the gate like I belonged there –

"And where," he said, "do you think you might be coming to."

"Well", I said "I was just coming to see Mr Ransom".

"Mr. Ransom is it?" he said, "and would you be having an appointment."

"Oh....Yes," I said.

"Well", he said, "you'd better be keeping it in London because that's where Mr. Ransom is, he's not on call today."

"Oh," I said, "Well, it doesn't matter – I'll see somebody else. I don't mind who I see."

"I know some in there who'd mind seeing you though", he said. "Look sonny a Fillum Studio is a very busy place, you can't have people just wandering around any old how. Now run away like a good boy, I'm busy.

"Couldn't I ... "

"No," he said.

"Well I .."

"No," he said.

So I went.

I didn't go far though.

Coming down the road was a gang of workmen carrying great long planks of wood – about twelve of them – two to a plank.

I whipped off my new collar, tied a hanky round my neck, stuffed my jacket under my shirt and pulled my hat well down.

As the last plank was going past me, I said to the man on the end, "give you a hand mate".

"Why?" he said, "you got one too many?"

"Just trying to be helpful", I said.

"All right", he said, "cop hold while I light a fag."

And so we went filing in. Morning Pat, - morning Pat, morning Pat – said the workmen – Morning Tom, Morning George, Morning Harry. Morning Pat, I said, looking the other way. Morning .... He looked up sharp – but by that time me and my end of the plank had gone.

I got tidied up in the cloakroom and began to wander down the long studio corridor. My collar was beginning to look like a bus ticket, but I still felt the world was my oyster – and have you ever tried to open an oyster? At the far end of the corridor I came to a door marked "Julius Caesar, Production Manager" This is it, I thought and I knocked and I went in. There was nobody there, but across the room was another door. So I banged on that.

"Come in" growled a voice, so in I went, and found myself in front of three men at a big desk.

"Well", said the one sitting in the middle.

"I've come about Julius Caesar", I said.

"Well," he said, "what can you tell us about Julius Caesar we don't already know".

"Nothing," I said, "I wondered if I could have an audition."

"You're a trifle young for the part son," he said.

"I'd be all right for Mark Anthony though", I said, "Friends – Romans – Countrymen.."

They stared at me – I went on

"Lend me your ears – I came to bury Caesar not to praise him – The evil that men do" – I banged on the desk.

"Is nothing to the evil you have done" said the man behind the desk looking down at the red ink trickling over his trousers from the bottle I'd upset. "Do you mind getting out of here."

Well, there wasn't much point in staying was there?

Two doors along the corridor was another office marked "Julius Caesar. Unit Manager".
Well I didn't know what a Unit Manager was but it sounded pretty important and in I went again.

"Yes?" said a big grey haired man who was looking through some papers.

"I've come about Julius Caesar", I said.

"Why – what's he done to you?"

"Nothing," I said, I'd just like an audition for a part.

"What part."

"Well, how about Brutus," I said.

"It's cast".

"Well, Casca or Cinna or Cassius."

"They're all cast Laddie – all I need is a clapper-boy" he said holding up one of those clapper boards they bang before every take in the Studios.

"Oh," I said, "I could do that honest, I could clap real loud, listen" – I picked up the board and shouted "Scene 103 Take 3." And I clapped the clapper hard, right across the nose of the Production Manager from along the corridor who'd just walked in without knocking. He didn't half look funny, but I didn't wait for the laugh.

And then right at the end of the corridor I found the right place at last. A door marked "Julius Caesar – Casting Manager". He was a nice chap, but he couldn't help much. The only parts that weren't cast were Caesar's wife and the old blind soothsayer.

"Well," I said, "In Shakespeare's time the women's parts were played by boys."

"Yes," he said, "but they were pretty boys," and he looked at me – and you couldn't call me pretty even in those days.

"But I could do the old blond soothsayer," I said. I closed my eyes and stretched out my hand --- "Caesar – Caesar Beware the Ides of March, Beware …."

And there stood the Production Manager with on of my fingers in each of his eyes.

As I ran out into the corridor I heard him shouting "Will somebody get that lunatic out of this Studio"

And I joined a long queue at the canteen door and was blowing my nose hard as they all came looking for me.

Well, I got into the canteen alright, but I felt pretty conspicuous sitting there watching everybody tucking into their mid-morning coffee and buns.

"What's the matter love," said a round little lady in a white overall who was clearing up the empties, "off your grub."

"No, as a matter of fact," I said, "I'm … I'm er.."

"Broke," she said.

"That's right," I said, "as a matter of fact I am a bit short of cash."

"Here love," she said, "have this with me then," and she got a mug of coffee and a Swiss bun and plonked them in front of me.

"Oh I don't like …."

"Don't worry," she said, "You'll earn it – you can help me get the tea trolley into the Studio and pour out while I take the money. There's an overall – put it on when you've done and we'll go."

And that was how I got into my first film set – on Stage One in Denwood Studios – pushing a tea trolley.

As soon as we got on to the Set a man called out –

"All right every-body – 10 minutes for tea."

I hardly had time to see what the Set looked like I was so busy pouring. And I was still at it when the same man shouted again

"All right everybody, here we go laugh and scratching – back to work everybody please."

"This English custom ruin-a my stomach, ruin-a my picture and cost a fortune in a breaks a-for-tea" said a tall thin man.

Who's that," I whispered to the canteen lady.

"Giuseppe Marco, the Director," she said.

"Now," he went on, "everybody-a finish having-a fun – we do-a some work – eh?

Where's the soldier who-a says Hail Caesar."

There was a silence.

"Where's the geezer who says Hail Caesar," said the assistant.
"Actually Charley," said a chap who must have been his assistant, "they sent a fellow down but he'd got the wrong head."

"Who's-a head he got then!?" shouted the Director.

"Actually sir," he said, "it was his own head but it was the wrong size."

"What's-a matter with the size?"

"It wouldn't fit the helmet sir."

"You mean-a we only got-a one helmet!!"

"Actually sir – yes. And it won't fit anyone we've got down here, actually."

"You mean-a we a-stand here doing a-nothing because-a nobody a-fit-a the helmet?"

Nobody said anything and everybody sort of looked somewhere else – except me.

And he spotted me alright. "You" he shouted. I went over. "Putta this on," he ordered. I did. He looked at me and then he grinned – "Here is the noblest Roman of them all," he said – "Can you say "Hail Caesar".

I took a deep breath.

"Hail Caesar," I shouted.

At that moment the Production Manager came on to the set.

"Get that lunatic out of here," he said.

"Whada you mean – get him out a here,?" Said the Director – "He plays the part.

You can hear-a what he says, his head's-a the right-a size – give him the helmet."

And they did – and I've kept it ever since.

NO SMOKE

When I was fourteen years old I was very small. I'm not that big now – they call me Shorty at work – but when I was fourteen I was very small for my age.

It had its advantages of course, for instance I travelled half fare on the trams right up to when I left school. That was how I saved the money to buy some cigarettes – my dad always gave me the full fare and I stuck to the difference.

My own cigarettes! That was something – I'd looked forward to it for years. You see I was so small nobody would ever chance letting me have one of theirs, not even my own pals after a game of knock-up football or cricket down in the brickyard. So one wet winter day, soon after I was fourteen, I got off the tram a couple of stops away from home, put me school cap in me pocket, left me satchel just outside on the pavement an walked very firmly into a tobacco-shop - well as firmly as I could up on the tips of my toes.

The tobacconist looked down at me from over the top of his high counter, "Helloh sonny", he said, "you're in the wrong shop - the sweetshop's next door". I didn't say a word - but I felt myself going red right down to the seat of my pants as I turned and went.

Out in the street the trams flamed past rocking with laughter, and all the people walking seemed to be looking at me and smiling and nudging each other. I couldn't stand it. I cut off along a side street, down the hill towards the brickyard. Half-way down, tucked in between two high houses, there was a narrow shop that sold old magazines, comics and cat-meat or swapped any one of them for the other. It was a favourite spot of all the kids in the neighbourhood. Miserably I stood looking through the window. Lumps of meat and big blue flies glittered in the light of a naphtha lamp and spread out below them on a shelf were the comics and mags. An occasional fly curiously exploring the rusty drippings from the meat above.

I saw all this with a blank eye. This was all I expected to see in this window, and I had seen it all a dozen times before. But the strange thing was that to-night I noticed for the first time a big placard at the back of the window advertising a brand of cigarettes. Maybe I noticed it this time for the first time because it was the first time I sought cigarettes. I didn't know old mother Jenkins sold cigarettes, and anyway, maybe she didn't. She was probably just using placard to shield the shop from the eyes of the window for some precious privacy of trade.

Still, I had no qualms about old Mother Jenkins, she and I were old friends.

"What have you brought me lad?" she said, as I went in.

"No swops tonight Mrs. Jenkins," I answered, "I want some fags."

"Oh," she said, "I don't know that I ought to sell 'em to small ones like you."

"Oh, don't worry," I told her, "they're for me dad."

So I got my cigarettes.

Then I didn't know what to do with them. Of course I had to smoke them, but where, how? Outside, what about the police? Inside, one boy had been sent away from school for smoking in the cloakroom. As I was thinking my feet took me automatically down the hill to the brick yard, where some other kids were playing football in the light of the gas lamps. Should I tell them my secret – no, they'd all want one and somebody was bound to split if everybody knew.

I was still trying to work it all out when one boy shouted "want a game – lend us your coat for a goal post and you can be goalie."

So I joined in; my coat, buttoned tight round four or five others, standing like a dwarf at my side on the damp ground, with the carton of cigarettes showing square in the pocket.

With the score at 17 all and the small boy who owned the ball already complaining that it was time he went home to supper, the outcry was terrific when the ball cannoned into my goal-post knocking it about 8 foot further into the brick yard, and the opponents claimed a goal. There was such a row that until we found that the small boy who wanted his supper had taken his ball and gone home, I did not notice that my goal-post had landed in a deep lorry rut full of water.

The cigarettes were saturated. Up in my bedroom after we had eaten, I spread them like sodden twigs on the table by my bed. One, slightly less wet than the rest, I tried to light. It oozed brief smoke and shreds of tobacco frayed into my mouth. It tasted terrible.

And I was ready to give up when I went to my school satchel to get out my homework. The satchel was standing against the left of a chair, facing my gas fire, and as I bent to get my books out I saw that the small front sac would make a perfect ledge for the cigarettes, high enough to get the full heat of the fire.

Carefully I propped the pappy tubes upright in front of the fire. The first five dried out and flaky and I set the others up in their place. And while they were cooking, I lit my first cigarette.

The dry paper flared alarmingly to start with and the tobacco crackled away so fast that I scarcely seemed to have tasted it before the cigarette was finished and the stub flicked out of my window. The second went almost the same way, though there was a hot feeling on my tongue now and at the back of my eyes. I managed to swallow quite a lot of the third one, which was probably why the fourth one made me feel quite decidedly sick. My room was heavy with smoke. It was hard to see across it. And what I could see was developing an odd tendency to expand and float before my eyes. Stubbornly I lit the fifth. Halfway through it I felt very ill indeed and sagged limply on to my bed as my room spun around me and suddenly went dark.

He next thing I knew, I was in my father's arms being carried down the stairs with a fierce crackling in my ears and my little room belching smoke behind me. The rest of the night was full of bells and hose pipes and men in helmets and waterproofs.

I was quite ill for several days. But on the morning I was going back to school, my father and I had breakfast together.

"Funny thing about the fire," he said, "the Fire Brigade people said that it looked as if it was caused by a cigarette. I told them it was impossible of course: there couldn't by any cigarettes in your room could there son?"

"No, dad," I said, "of course not."

Well it was nearly true: there never have been since.

PUSHING THE BOAT OUT

This is the story of a lifebuoy with a hole in it.

I came by it years ago, when I was in a Concert Party on the Pier at the seaside.

It was a lovely summer and it was a nice little seaside town. And one of the things they were very proud of in this town was the boating pool. It was a very big pool that children used to sail their model yachts and tugs and steamers and motor boats and just plain bits of wood on.

The pool was quite near the pier and it backed on to a big car-park where the charabancs that brought the day trippers, used to wait. And it was just a short cut for me on my way home for tea between the concert we gave in the afternoon and the one in the evening.
Of course by the time we'd finished the first concert and got our make-up off most of the

children were home for tea and most of the charabancs had left on their long journeys home and the pool was deserted; so I was a bit surprised one day to find a little boy at the boating pool just pushing his boat around the edge. He was all alone, and he wasn't really having much luck with his boat – he just didn't seem to be able to get it really going out across the middle of the pond.

It was a jolly nice little boat and I could see that it could do better things than just scrape around the edge butting its bowsprit into the concrete and barking its keel on the steps.

So I went up to him and I said "Nice little boat you've got there. Can't you get it to go out?"

"No," he said, "No I ……"

"Oh, that's a pity," I said, before he could finish. "Here let me help you."

"Well," he said, "I'm not ……"

"Not very good at it, eh? I said, Right come, I'll show you how to send a boat off on a voyage of adventure."
And I set the sails and fixed the rudder, and I felt the wind on my forefinger, gave her a push and off she went. She sailed away into the

middle of the pond swift as a gull. Then quite suddenly, the tights sails slackened and fluttered and hung loose and aimless at the mast. And the swift little ship bobbed gently out there completely becalmed.

"What's the matter?" Said the boy.

"Wind's dropped," I said, "don't worry, it'll fresh again and she'll come sailing home – we'd best get round the other side."

Off we went round the pond, but the boat just stayed out there in the middle, bobbing and dipping to us like a lady-in-waiting at a Royal Wedding.

"I hope she comes in soon," said the little boy, "I've got to go home."

"Oh, don't worry," I said, "it won't be long – where've you got to get to?"

"London," he said.

"London!!"

"Yes, you see, I came for the day on a ……"
He didn't need to tell me; before he'd finished, a very big lady with a big round jolly face that was all red except where the sun had peeled

the skin off her nose, popped over the fence between the pool and the car-park and called out: "Harry – come on, the chara's going."

"I can't Ma," he called back, "me boat's gone."

"Where's it gone?" She shouted.

"In the middle," he said.

"I told you not to send it in the middle, didn't I?" she said.

"I didn't Mum," said Harry, "it was this man."

"Ho," she said, "was it." And with that she was over the fence. "What's the idea young man" she said to me, "taking young Harry's boat away from him."

"Well," I said, "I didn't take it away from him."

"Oh," she said, "then what's it doing out there?"

"It sailed out there," I said.

"And how could it sail out there if you didn't push it?"
"Well," I said, "it had a bit of wind."

"Are you trying to be funny," she said. "Here," she went on to the crowd that was gathering round the car-park fence – "Here, listen to this sauce box, takes a kid's boat away from him, loses it in the middle of the water and then says it wasn't his fault."

There was a grumble from the crowd and quite a lot of them climbed over the fence.

"Look," I said, "I didn't know the wind was going to drop, did I?"

"Well," said a man in a bus-driver's cap, "whether you knew it or not, you'd better pick it up quick, my chara's leaving in five minutes with or without the wind behind it."

Little Harry started to cry "Mum – I want me boat".

"Don't worry lovey," she said, "you'll have it, now come on young man what are you going to do?"

"That's right," said the people behind her, "what are you going to do?"

"Well," I said, "if you'll give me your address I could always send it on."
  "That's a likely tale," said Mum, "when your ship comes in I suppose."

And everybody laughed at that.

"Well," I said, "I'll pay you for it if you like."

"That's better," said the bus-driver. "And hurry up, I'm leaving any minute now."

"But I can't do it now, I don't happen to have any money on me."

"Chuck him in after it," said a voice from the back of the crowd.

"That's right," said somebody else.

"That's enough of that," said Mum, "we don't want any bullying. Young man," she said, "if you're anything of a sort you'll wade in and get our Harry's boat for him so's he can catch the chara' and go home happy."

"All right," I said, "I will." And I rolled up my trousers as far as they'd go, and I began to wade out to the boat that was still bobbing about in the middle.

Now at that time I couldn't swim – and after a few paces I began to get worried, because I found that the boating pool sloped down very fast and was soon very deep – practically up to my shoulders and I was still miles from the boat.

"Hey," I shouted, "I'll be out of my depth in a moment – throw me a lifebuoy. I can't swim."

Somebody hooked one off the stand at the side of the pool and ringed me with it. "Thanks" I shouted, and I pushed on. It wasn't cold, and by now my clothes were in such a mess it didn't matter any more.

The funny thing was that as I pushed father out, the water seemed to get shallower, not deeper. And it wasn't till I looked back to the people standing on the side that I realised what was happening – for I could see the water was lower now at the edge of the pool too – the water was emptying away!!

Every now and again they empty the pool and refilled it with fresh water – and this was one of the 'nows'.

The water was emptying very fast indeed, and there was a sort of whirlpool now in the middle of the pond and the boat was spinning around in it like a top. The water was gurgling and sucking away and I was splashing across now as fat as I could go with it slopping at my feet. And as I got to the middle and reached down for the boat – Verlupp – it was sucked away from under my hand like the tongue of a toad.

I couldn't believe it at first that I heard Mum's voice – "Well, you'll have to buy our Harry another one now, young man." There was quite a crowd standing around the edge now, and they all seemed to agree with Mum.

But before I could say anything there was a huge whoooosh right underneath me and a great spout of fresh water caught me right in the seat of my soaking trousers.

The water was coming back in. And I remembered it would be deep, so I struggled into the lifebuoy – it was a children's lifebuoy so it was quite a struggle, and I'd just about got into it, with the water lopping round my waist, when there under my nose I saw Harry's boat bobbing away like a cork, none the worse for it's submarine trip.

I grabbed it and struggled my way to the edge. Harry grabbed it from me, and
'Thanks young man," said Mum, and "Come along now – all aboard" said the driver of the charabanc and off they all went and left me, standing there in the water with the lifebuoy round me like first prize on a hoop-la stand.
I'll never know how I managed to get into that ring, panic I suppose, but I certainly couldn't get out of it. And I felt such a fool walking along the street like a flying saucer until I

found somebody to saw it off me – I had to pay
for it of course, and I've kept it ever since.

Hole an' all.

RICH SEEDS

Have you ever eaten a pomegranate? Strange fruit aren't they, with their leathery cases, bitter pith and thousands of pips. Always seems a lot of work for that little piece of scenty-sweet fruit.

I saw them growing once, in Tangier, just after the War. I'd been out in those parts doing troop shows and I thought I'd have a look around before I went home.

Tangier hot, smelly and international. Tangier was a free zone, and that meant that practically anything went – any currency, any nationality, any kind of business – And a lot of it was very funny business.

Among all the honest traders and bankers and business men, there were nearly as many rogues and vagabonds and smugglers - smuggling was practically a local industry.

As a matter of fact after a couple of days I was beginning to feel a bit disappointed. Walking round Tangier wasn't all that different from walking round some of the seedier parts of London at lunch-time.

But it was just on lunch time, on the third day, when a chap in a full Arab outfit bumped flat into me in a little market street – said in very good English "the pomegranate seeds – Doctor.."

And then just as I was going to explain that I wasn't a doctor, he slid very gently to a heap at my feet and I saw the knife sticking in his back.

Of course everybody started milling around and giving advice but by the time the police arrived he was quite dead. And I was taken along to Police Headquarters to make a statement. And that wasn't as easy as I thought.

"I was walking along," I said, "and this man came up to me and said 'pomegranate seeds doctor.' "

"Ah" – said the Chef de Police – "he is a friend of yours when he lives?"

"Oh no," I said, "never seen him before."

"Then how does he know you are doctor?"

"I'm not a doctor."

"That's serious."

"What's serious?"

"Pretending to be a doctor."

"I've never pretended to be a doctor."

"Then why he calls you Doctor Seeds?"

"It was pomegranate seeds."

"Alright, Doctor Pomegranate Seeds."

Well, believe it or not we got it sorted out and I left the Police station a fairly free man.

I'd gone a couple of blocks on my way back to my hotel when I realised I was not alone. All of a sudden there were three of us and the other two were much bigger than me. One of them had his hand on my back and was prodding me along with his finger –

"D'you mind taking your finger out of my ribs," I said. "That's not my finger chum," he said, and pushed a bit harder. I felt something prick the skin of my back.

"Well," I said, "you've got jolly long fingernails, I'll come quietly."

And he put the knife away in his pocket and took my arm.

We went to a little hotel off the back street I'd never seen before. And in a bare room that had just a couple of beds in it they started talking.

"Who paid you to kill Ibrahim? Where's the stuff?"

"Gentlemen," I said, "one question at a time. I didn't kill anybody."

"I see – people just lie at your feet with knives in their backs."

"Oh," I said, "so that was Ibrahim."

"Maybe they should have introduced you first, it's not nice to kill a man you don't know."

"Look," I said, "I didn't kill him – he just came up to me and said 'pomegranate seeds – Doctor' ... and fell down."

"How'd he know you were a doctor?"

"Now don't you start," I said – "you are English aren't you?"

"Yes," he said – "so are you, that's a de-mob suit if ever I saw one."

"Hey wait a minute," said the other chap – "maybe Ibrahim saw that too, that's why he tried to speak to you – What's your name?" he asked me – I told him.

"Well I'm Jim Mace and this is Dick Hart. Look here Johnny," he said, "you're in something you didn't ask for."

And as he said it the water jug on the other side of the room seemed to jump into the air and throw itself on the ground with a crash – the two men threw me on the ground with a crash too and they kept me down there under the bed in a puddle of water. I lay there while they jumped either side of the window and swung the blinds shut. Then I got up slowly.

"Somebody obviously thinks you know something that they don't want made public," said Jim, pointing to the bullet that had buried itself in the wall.

"I see," I said; "well, if I ask nicely do you think I could get out of this thing I didn't ask to get into?"

"I doubt it," he said, "you know too much."

"Too much!" I said, "I don't even know what you're talking about."

"Well," he said, "you might as well get shot knowing, as not knowing. You've heard of the Park Lane Rubies?"

"Yes," I said, "they were stolen in England a few weeks ago."

"That's right," he said – "50 of them, beautifully matched stones, worth a fortune, and the insurance company are paying us to get them back. We've traced them to Tangier and Ibrahim was one of the crooks – I suppose they fell out, because he was on his way to double cross his chums for the reward when he copped it."

"When I copped it you mean," I said.

"That's right son," he said, " `cos you're in it now – neck high. Now come tell us again – what did Ibrahim say?"

All he said was "Pomegranate Seeds … Doctor"

"Well, that doesn't help much does it – about half the population of Tangier grows their own pomegranates and as for "Doctor" – that just don't make sense. Come on – let's go and have a bite to eat."

We left the hotel and walked along for a bit in silence.

"I wonder," I said ….

"Sh-sh," said Jim, "keep quiet and think, just concentrate, something's bound to come to us."

It did.

A big black car came hurtling round the corner at about sixty miles an hour and came straight at us. We dived for a doorway.

"I wish you wouldn't say things like that," I said to Jim.

The quiet man spoke for the first time. "I bust my wrist" he said.

We hopped into a taxi and got him to the hospital. After a bit we were shown into a surgery, and the doctor was going over the wrist when a nurse came in and said – "your chauffeur has brought the fruit doctor – shall we deal with it as usual?"

"Yes," he said, still busy at his work, "the children's ward first eh?"

"Yes doctor," she said, and went.

"The children love my pomegranates," he said as he finished strapping up the wrist – "There, I think that will do – it is not as serious as it feels."

"You grow pomegranates, do you Doctor?" I asked.

"Yes," he said, "but then of course everybody does here, but I pride myself mine are rather special."

"I bet they are," I said, "I'd like to see them."

"Yes," he said, "you must come along some time." And with that he ushered us out.

"Hah!" I said – "some time – never, he means."

"Doesn't matter what he means," said Jim, "we're paying him a visit – it's a long shot worth trying."

It wasn't hard to get the Doctor's address. And the next morning, very early we went visiting. He had a nice little estate on the outskirts of Tangier and we browsed around his grounds for quite a while – I don't know whether we expected to find a bunch of rubies dangling from a pomegranate tree – until suddenly we found two black dogs with long white teeth, and an Arab with a gun.

That was the end of our browsing. The dogs and the Arab and the gun and us all went into the house to see the doctor.

"Well gentlemen," he said, "you should have let me know you were coming – such an ungracious welcome. It is all right Abdullah you may go. –"

We felt better after that. The doctor chatted with us and we all had coffee, and we were beginning to think that our long shot was way off target when a pretty little blond girl with

- 258 -

pig-tails came bouncing in. "Daddy," she said, "can I help pick some fruit?"

"Yes my dear of course," he said, "ask Abdullah."
"Abdullah never lets me," she said, "where's Ibrahim Daddy? he lets me."

"Ibrahim is no longer with us my dear," he said.

"Oh well," she said, "it'll have to be Abdullah." And she danced out.

None of us said anything for a moment.

"Pity about Ibrahim wasn't it?" I said.

"Possibly," he said, "but you know with Arab servants they come and they go."

We looked at each other a while.

"Ibrahim went a bit further than most, didn't he?" I said.

"I don't know where Ibrahim went," he answered, "but I must go. Gentlemen stay as long as you wish, enjoy the gardens and the pomegranates."

"Ugly looking things aren't they?" I said, picking up one that lay on a dish by itself.

"Only the outside," said the doctor, "the sweet red fruit inside is priceless - and good for the health. Excuse me" – he took the pomegranate from me – "this I must take for a special patient."

And off he went – leaving us wondering what to do next and looking at the pomegranate trees.

"The sweet red fruit inside is priceless". I muttered.

"That's it!" Said Jim.

"What's it?" I said.

"That's it – that's where they are – priceless fruit - those rubies are in a pomegranate."

"Alright," I said – "there's only about half a million there – you start looking!"

"Come on," he said, pulling me out into the garden.

"You must be cracked," I said, "if you think I'm going to ..."

"You're going to the hospital," he said, "so am I, come on!"

We got into the children's ward just as the Doctor finished sounding a little Arab boy's chest.

He stood up and took of his stethoscope as we arrived.

He didn't say anything to us but turned to the little boy.

"That's fine Ahmed," he said, "you'll soon be well. Here, I brought this for you," and from the loose pocket of his white overall he took the pomegranate.

"Wait a minute Doctor," I said, "isn't this is a little indigestible for a sick boy?" and I took the pomegranate. As I pressed on it with my fingers it split open and out came a stream of priceless, ruby, fruit.

The insurance company was very generous, but I still don't like pomegranates!

A HEAD FULL OF WISHES

This is one of those stories that is very difficult to believe, but I know it's true – see what you think.

I'll tell you one thing right away – I own a wig that I wouldn't wear again if you paid me – I just keep it around so's nobody else can get into trouble.

I wore it as one of the footmen in Cinderella about twenty Xmases ago. There were eight of us footmen it was a very posh pantomime, at a big theatre, right in the middle on London. You couldn't miss it, it had a bank on one side of it and a pawnbroker's on the other – we always used to say, we put our money in the one when we got paid on Friday and our valuables in the other when we were broke on Monday.

Still we were young then and we had fun. The eight of us shared a cubby-hole under the stage – they called it dressing room – though there wasn't room in it for one of the mice to dress in, let alone eight footmen. There was no door, no windows, no water and it was just curtained off from the orchestra pit, so the musicians used it as a short cut, and when they started playing we could hardly hear ourselves talk.

Well, one night, the orchestra had just pushed their way through as usual and we were settling down again, like a rush hour tube when it leaves the station – and Harry, the bloke who shared my chair – there was only room for four chairs, so we had half each and switched round when it got uncomfortable – Harry turned to me and said:

"Here Johnny, somebody's in my trousers,"

I said, "Don't be daft there's hardly room for you in them by yourself". I was busy making up at the time.

"No," he said, "I haven't got 'em on"

"Well", I said, "put 'em on – this is Cinderella not a strip tease".

"Oh, shut up," he said, "don't you understand? they've gone. I had 'em right here till the orchestra pushed through, now they've gone".

"Well," I said, "one of the band boys must have nicked them, go and have a look."

I was right – they were there in the orchestra pit draped over the harp like old laundry – and you should have heard the audience roar with laughter as Harry climbed through the pit to get 'em, in his little short pants.

"Rotten lot", he said, as he came struggling back – "did you see who took 'em Johnny?"

"No", I said, as I was getting my wig settled nice and tight on my head – "No, I wish I'd spotted him though."

And we thought no more about it. Not even the next night when we heard that the bassoon player couldn't turn up because he had a nasty dose of measles – "Spots! Spots like half a crowns," one of his pals said.

That night, after the first act, we were kicking our heels till we went on again. I was just checking my wig was still on straight, when I said, "I wish we could get away early tonight, I promised to meet my mum from her evening classes."

"Evening classes," Harry said, "what's she learning."

"Cookery," I said.

"Bit late isn't it," he said.

"Yes," I said, "she used to cook fine when she just guessed, it's terrible now she measures everything. And we don't like her going home alone half across London."

Well the curtain hadn't been up for more than a couple of minutes, when the Stage Manager walked on and stopped the action of the pantomime and said to the audience:
"Ladies and gentlemen, a small fire has broken out in the bar at the back of the Stalls. There is absolutely no need for panic, the Fire Service is arriving now" – we could hear the bells as he said it – "but please would you all leave quietly by the side exits".

So everybody went home early, in fact I had to wait for my mother's evening class to finish.

I suppose it was the next night that the penny began to drop. It was a dirty night, pouring with rain – we could hear it beating on the roof over the stage and when the show was over our street clothes were still wet from getting to the theatre.

"What a night," I said to Harry as I was taking off my wig, "I wish I had my car calling for me so's I could just lay back in luxury all the way home."

Well – I did lay back in luxury all the way home – in an ambulance. I fell down the three steps to the stage door and they thought I'd bust my leg at first. It was just a bad sprain, but they still sent me home from the hospital in an ambulance.

And as I lay in bed for the next couple of days I got to thinking about that fire and the bassoon player and my long ride home. When I got back to the theatre, I had a word with Harry about it.

"Harry," I said, "do you believe that some people have special powers?"

"You mean like policemen".

"No," I said, "I mean like ..... well magic."
He looked at me – "here Johnny," he said, "I thought it was your leg you fell on, not your head."

I said, "All right, be funny, but every time I wish for something it happens."

"I suppose you wished for a sprained ankle?" he said. "No," I said, "but I wished for a luxury ride home and I got it. And what about that fire stopping the show when I wished I could get away early? and that bassoon player's measles?"

"Don't tell me you've got measles?" he said.

"No," I said, "but when you said that somebody in the orchestra pit had pinched your trousers, I said I wished I'd spotted him – and he got measles!"

Harry looked at me for a bit. Then: "All right," he said, wish for something now."

I'd finished my make up, wig an' all, while we were talking, and was just getting into my footman's uniform. "All right," I said, "what shall I wish for?"

"What do you want?" he said.

"Well," I said, "I wish I had a big fat leading part in a first class show."

We didn't have time to see if it worked, because the Stage Manager came dashing in and shouted: "Any of you boys ever played Dame?"

"Well," I said, "I played Cinderella's step-mother in Rep once."

"You're the very boy then," he said, "come on – our step-mother's been in a car crash."

"What about his understudy," I said.

"He was in the other car," said the Stage Manager. "Come on, look lively."

Well, I didn't make a bad go of it – in fact by Act 3, I was enjoying myself. I found I knew most of the part from watching the rehearsals, and it wasn't all that different from the way I played it in the repertory company. When it was over, all the bosses thanked me very much and told me that I could play the part until one of the others was fit to come back, and that wasn't very likely to happen as it was a pretty bad car crash.

So I was really cock a hoop when I got back to our cubbyhole under the stage.

The other seven footmen were waiting for me. "Gentlemen," I said, "look enviously upon me – no longer will I huddle below stairs with you menials – you are looking at the newest Dame on the London stage."

"Johnny," said Harry, "I told them."

"Told 'em what?" I said.

"About you and your magic."

"Oh" – I said – "that ….." As a matter of fact I'd forgotten about it in the excitement.

"Go on Johnny," they said, "do some more."

I thought for a minute – then I said – "No".

"Why not" they shouted.

"Well," I said, "it's a funny thing, but when-ever I wish for anything – I seem to get it – but something seems to go wrong on the way – measles – fires – car-crashes."

"Well," they said, "Don't make it a very special wish – just an ordinary little one – go on Johnny – show us."

"Oh …. all right," I said, "just a little wish then …I wish …. I wish I had a cup of tea." We all waited - but nothing happened.

I felt a bit of a fool. "oy," I said, "what's the matter with you wherever you are – I WISH I HAD A CUP OF TEA."

But nothing happened. The boys really took the Mickey out of me. They didn't stay long though, they were all dressed and ready to go while I'd been talking to the people upstairs, and soon they went.

"Well," I said to Harry, "I don't care." I picked up the wig. I won't have to wear this tatty old thing any more anyway. And I slung it into the corner. Just as the Stage Manager came in.

"Take it easy with the props Johnny," he said – picking up the wig – "you'll be needing this. The big boy says we must get another star-name to play the Dame."

"I thought the big boys said I could play it," I said.

"Yes," he said, "but this is the really big boy – the man who puts up all the money. Sorry Johnny boy, the new man takes over to-morrow – if you want to stay with us you can still be the footman." And he tossed me back the wig.

"Thanks," I said, "thanks for ......"

But he was gone already, and we were alone in the theatre.

"Money," I said, "Money!!" I shoved the wig on my head angrily – "I wish I was sitting on a load of money."

The next thing I knew I was ten foot down sitting in a pool of golden sovereigns and bells were ringing all round me.

Above me I could see Harry's scared face peering through the hole in the floor where I'd been sitting. "Where am I," I mumbled.

"Coo," he said, "you must be in the vault of the bank next door".
At that moment a heavy iron door at my side swung back and I was surrounded by policemen. Me and Harry spent the night in gaol. It was next morning before we could get in touch with anybody to prove that we had a right to be in the theatre so late and that we weren't robbing the Bank.

I carried on playing the footman, but I made them change my wig. I've kept it ever since, of course, for safety, but I've never worn it again.

YOU HAVE BEEN WARNED

Have you ever seen a bloke really scared. I mean nervy right down to the knuckles? Well I hadn't 'til I went into a café in the Balls Pond Road for a cuppa on the way home from work one evening.

This feller comes along with his cup in his hand and sits down next to me. His hands shaking so much he slops his tea into my lap.

"Here, take it easy cocker," I said.

"Sorry chum," he said, "sorry." And he sat there sucking on an unlit dog-end and picking the tobacco off his lip.

Well, I could only stand so much of that. "Look," I said, "d'you want to smoke that thing or pluck it?"

"Eh?" he said, "Oh – got a match mate?"

I gave him a box. He dropped half of 'em on the table, kept one and rattled the rest like a rumba band.

"Here," I said, "let me do it for you." I lit the fag and he sucked so hard on it, it burnt right down to his lip on the one draw. "Now take it easy, I said, nothing can be as bad as the way you're behaving – pull yourself together."

"What for?" he said, "what's the good, what's the good of anything? Look, you listen to me: I'm in the sewers see. The very deep ones, about a couple of hundred feet down under Westminster, that's my beat. That's how it is in the sewers, the better you are the lower you do. Well I've been working in the sewers all my life and I've just about reached the bottom, that means I'm at the top. Well, I was having a final check along the tunnels and pipes about 4 o'clock this morning, when I come over all funny – sort of dopey-sleepy feeling. Aye-aye, I said to meself 'fumes' – watch it Harry boy. And I scarpered as quick as I could back to the main conduit. But nothing showed on any of the dials

– pressure was up, flow was normal, everything as it should be. Just a false alarm, must have been me, I thought. I was due off at five, so it wasn't worth going back along the alleys. I had a last check over the gauges and dials and switches – marked them O.K. in the day book and came up at our point just south of Charing Cross.

It was a lovely clear starry night, with the morning just beginning to milk the sky. There was no sound and no movement as I walked across Trafalgar Square. The pigeons weren't posing and the starlings were still. I hung around at Cambridge Circus for a bus to the Angel, but none came so I started walking. I got all the way to Holborn Hall before I saw any signs of life – if you could call it life. There was a trolley bus at the lights. The lights were green, but the bus wasn't moving and there was no sound from the motor. I crossed over and looked up into the driver's cabin. The driver was just sitting there – leaning forward, one hand releasing the hand brake and the other on the steering wheel.

"What are you waiting for mate?" I said, "the lights won't get any greener."

He didn't answer me, just sat there like something out of a wax works. Must have gone off his nut, I thought, so I went round the back to chat to the conductor. He was standing on his platform talking to the only passenger, sitting just inside. You could see he was talking to him, but there weren't any words. There wasn't any sound at all, and as I got closer I saw that his lips weren't moving, they were just parted and he had one eyebrow cocked like he was asking "fourpenny workman?" And the passenger was sitting there grinning, leaning over a bit, with his hand in his pocket.

"Here," I said, "you'd better get weaving or you'll have the Inspector on you tail." The conductor didn't answer me. And somehow I didn't expect him to. My voice sounded like I was talking in a fur lined room – it couldn't have reached him even if he could have heard it.

By now, I was beginning to get scared. I cut back towards Westminster, I reckoned somebody ought to tell the Prime Minister, or somebody, what was going on. It was getting quite light as I crossed the Lincoln's Inn Fields. Light, quiet and still. No birds sang, the air didn't move and the trees stood like cut-outs in a pantomime. Round Bush House, down the Strand and up Whitehall, cars, coppers and cleaners, birds, buses and barrow boys, pinned in action like butterflies on a board. There wasn't even a ripple on the river.

When I got to the House of Commons I was scared and sweating. I ran up the steps, with my head well down, I didn't want to look at anything anymore. That was how I nearly fell over the little chap sitting on the top step.

"Oh," I said, "sorry."

He looked up at me. He had a funny big domey head with no hair on it. And eyes that seemed to be looking at you through thick glasses. He wore a plain tunic and a sort of kilt and his arms and legs dangled out all rubbery, like they had no bones or joints. "Ah," he said, looking at me, "did we miss you?" His voice was high and soft – like air in a tin whistle before you hit a note. "Perhaps it's as well," he went on, "our communication might be the more effective if conveyed by word of mouth. Now listen carefully. Your earth scientists have been worried recently about the disposal of their radio-active waste materials. It occurred to one of them that a huge container mounted on to a rocket ship and directed into outer space might be an excellent solution to the problem. Once beyond Earth's gravitational pull, the container full of radio-active waste would circle the Earth as a minute satellite, to the end of time.

The idea was approved and the rocket was launched. Unfortunately nobody had considered the possibility of the rocket, in outer space and beyond Earth's gravitational pull, reaching the gravitational pull of some other planet. Well, it did – our planet in fact, and it has caused us considerable inconvenience. Now this must stop – we have no desire that Earth should become an object of animosity. Our only wish is to live at peace with the Universe. To this end we have demonstrated our power by bringing to this great Earth Metropolis to a standstill. No ill effects will be felt from this, and life will now commence from precisely the point at which we stopped it. But I must urge you to convey our warning to an Earth Leader. Should another Radio Active Rocket fly into our orbit we may be forced to bring all life on Earth to a standstill."

Before I could say a word, he went, I didn't see him go anywhere, he just sort of dissolved. And suddenly it was dark again and I found myself standing there with Big Ben bashing out 5 o'clock right over my head.

Well since then I've been trying to get somebody to believe me. I got as far as the secretary to the Under Secretary to the Minister of Scientific Agriculture, at the House of Commons, but his and his secretary and the head porter, the hall porter, the door porter and this copper on the beat outside, all said I must have dreamt it. I've tried the House of Lords, the Old Bailey and No.10 Downing Street, but I can't see anybody and anybody I *do* see says I must have gone to sleep in my sewer and I shouldn't read horror comics. And that's all I've done all day."

He stopped talking and the two of us sat there in the café looking at our cups of cold tea. He looked up at me – "I s'pose you think I dreamed it too, eh?" he said.

"Well," I said, "yes, as a matter of fact I do – Are you quite sure you didn't?"

"I don't know," he said, "I don't know anything anymore. Maybe I did dream it. But then .... what's going to happen to us all if it wasn't a dream? Have you seen the papers? There's another Radio-active Waste Rocket going off to-night!"

THE WORD IS PEACE (Shalom)

I didn't want to spend that Christmas in Jerusalem. I may have been wrong, of course, because I didn't. But you can sometimes feel these things.

Back then, all the year round Jerusalem was divided. The high, white wall of the old Arab city sliced it off from Israel's Jerusalem like the pronged spine of some prehistoric monster. And come Christmas the prongs seemed to bristle as if one half was getting ready to celebrate and the other determinedly not.

The street outside the broadcasting station in Jerusalem, where I'd been working, was as narrow as a flute and the wind was whistling down it at four o'clock of the morning I left. That was six days before Christmas. My last recording for the American network was finished and all I had to do was say goodbye to some dozen friends around the city and catch a taxi into the port of Haifa at eight o'clock.

The sun came up through the bottom of my twelfth glass of brandy and lit my twelfth farewell. I stayed lit all the way to Haifa and some of the way out of it. Anyway, the Mediterranean was slapping the boat like a masseur in a Turkish bath when I woke up for breakfast on what proved to be December 20th.

Don't let's exaggerate this thing. A good percentage of that sleep was sheer exhaustion – I'd been working at Jerusalem tempo – that's about nineteen hours a day – filming, writing and broadcasting for three months. And I'm a sleepy sailor at the best of times – I need a great rolling sea to toss me out of my bunk.

I got it. All the way to Genoa.

Mark you, I like it that way if I've got a cabin to myself and I had. For that matter I had pretty well the whole ship to myself – social activity degenerated from a table of bridge, through three-handed poker to 'snap' with the radio operator – he had to stay above deck!

We docked in Genoa, on the twenty-third, to unload a cargo of grapefruit, and the wind came down from the heights above the city and slashed us with a cold bead-curtain of sleet.

I got a shore-pass and wandered around the market streets that run close to the docks, eating hot fried whitebait and some sort of thick crisps out of Newspaper – it wasn't quite up to a bob's worth of rock salmon and chips, like I'd eat back home, and I couldn't read the newspaper of course, but then you couldn't walk down Petticoat Lane drinking a bottle of Grappa, could you?

The market streets slope steeply and the icy rain turned them into shallow, rushing rivers with strange craft, like paper bags, trilby hats and orange peel, whipping downstream before the wind. Everybody had wet feet, cold hands, frost-nipped noses - and a strange hilarity of the heart. Come what may it was soon to be Christmas; and I was going to be home for it too. I realised that for the first time and began to share the joke against the weather like the crowd around me.

I drifted back to the ship in an aura of gladness and joy and beamed on the first officer like a visiting lighthouse as he picked his way towards me through the passengers at the rail. Quite a lot of passengers, all gazing greenly at the pleasant land, were taking their first fresh air in three days, while the boat was standing heavenly still.

He got to me. "You have somebody to meet," he said.

"No," I said, "but don't worry, I'm quite happy by myself."

He was a tidy little man, shining with shaving soap and gold braid. He sort of held up his hand for silence, like a schoolmaster, while he worked it out in Hebrew and then re-translated what he wanted to say.

"Here is somebody you have to meet. Mrs Nadlin was sure you would be obliged."

Well, I must say, Mrs Nadlin had been very obliging during my visit. She was the Haifa agent of the society for whom I'd been working is Israel. It was undoubtedly she who'd seen me safely on board three days before. "Surely," I said "she's done all she can for me now."

"Yes, now it is you for her." Well, that possibly wasn't quite the way he wanted to say it but it was certainly what he wanted to say. "Come, please" he went on, so I went.

We ended up two decks down, in third class. It was the same as first class, only there were more people sharing the same amount of space. There were four ladies in the cabin at which we tapped and entered and it was pretty full of those four ladies before we went in. Even the first officer must have got the feeling that there wasn't room for him on his own ship – he just said "this is Ruth" and shot off as if he'd gone down the wrong stairs at a public bath.

I looked round. "Nein" said the lady in the top left. "Non" said the lady in the top right. "Lo, lo" came from the bottom right and nothing at all from the bottom left, so I tried there. "Ruth?" I said – I scarcely recognised the name as I said it – out there it starts with the purr of a contented cat and then makes a noise like a cote full of doves – Hhhrrrooooth. Still she got what I meant: "Ken!" No, she wasn't mistaking me for anyone else, that's Hebrew for "Yes".

She looked like a child, sitting there on the edge of the bunk – with light brown hair, a nose that tipped sharply, like a cinema seat smothered in freckles and a wide mouth with no make-up on it.

"Mrs Nadlin said …."

Mrs Nadlin was a common factor and as I mentioned her name the three ladies told me, in three languages, and in chorus, what Mrs Nadlin had said – or what it was their guess that she'd said. Anyway, that was my guess at what they were saying. Ruth said nothing.

Eventually, I elected the lady who spoke French as the chief interpreter. She was a very fat lady and too polite to put her teeth in while I was there. Muted conversation with Ruth, in Hebrew, was translated into muffled French. Slowly I cottoned that the girl was going to London and Mrs Nadlin had told her that she'd ask me to keep an eye on her from Marseilles to Victoria.

"Elle est le bébé." the fat lady said

"Yes," I agreed, "she is a bit young for travelling alone."

"Non, non – elle *et* le bébé – elle a-t un enfant."

"She's got a baby!" I said. "Where? Did she nick it from an orphanage or something?"

"My baby." Said Ruth suddenly, quite loudly and clearly. She produced a bundle of lacy wool and held it up to me. I took hold of it and nearly dropped it back into her lap as it squeaked. It began to cry and the four of them looked at me as though I was a murderer.

"I see," I said, "well ....That's fine. I'll be glad to, er ...er... see you later, eh?"

As he saw me coming into the saloon, the first officer turned to the bar-tender. I got to him just as my tot came up. "Good Health" he said, lifting his glass. I took mine and agreed with him. Then I bought him one. He took it with a sort of apologetic look.

"Here's to Christmas in London," I said.

He didn't drink but looked more apologetic. "No." He said.

"Not for you maybe."

"No." He said.

"What do you mean 'no'?"

"Grapefruit."

"I don't care if there's no grapefruit," I said. "I'll be satisfied with Turkey, Christmas pud. and a couple of mince pies."
"Cannot unload grapefruit in this weather. Late leaving Genoa."

It percolated. "You mean no London for Christmas?"

"Yes," he said. "No."

"We'll miss the connection, eh?"

"Yes," he said. "No connections."

"Well," I said, "you're a help. First you give me a baby to take home, two babies come to think of it. Then you tell me I can't get home."

"Not me – the weather."

So it had the last laugh, the weather. And it must have laughed its head off the next day, when we sailed out of Genoa in a flat calm, under a warming sun. I went below and collected Ruth and the baby. The three of us watched the miles cream away under the bows of the ship. Ruth could speak English after all – It was weird but it was English, although she was shy of it. She'd learnt it from her husband, who was from London, and had been evacuated to Wales during the war, which gave her quite a dialect. His parents had been killed in the Blitz on the East End. Ruth herself was a Sabra – born in Israel that is - and named after a type of prickly cactus – and she and her husband had met and married while working on a kibbutz.

Now she was taking the baby to show him to her remaining in-laws.

The baby was very new and I was almost better than she was at handling him. After all, I had two to my credit and on a kibbutz parents get on with other work while babies are looked after by those whose job it is. I felt like Drake, or Stout Cortez, or somebody like that as I nursed him into Marseilles.

I didn't feel quite so heroic in the hotel, near the station, where we settled in to pass the time until the train for Calais left very early on Christmas morning. We were the only 'guests' and the manager didn't take kindly to us at all. To him, our passports were plainly at odds with our circumstances. To him, the sight of me showing Ruth the English way of changing a nappy was scarcely logical; and the French are so logical.

By the evening the baby was very unhappy and his unhappiness echoed around the empty dining-room. Ruth thought it may be due to her own discomfort on the voyage from Haifa, which seemed logical enough even for the French; so I by-passed the manager and found my way to the kitchens.

"Have you got any milk," I said, "powdered, for babies?" The chef looked at me as though I was barmy.

"Du lait – poudre? Pour les enfants. Les enfants nouveax né." I said. I don't know how good the French was but he got what I meant. What's more he had got what I needed. It was an English brand, and as I was the only one who could read English, I had to mix it, and I thanked Heaven for the English nanny who had left it, 'en passant'.

I couldn't guarantee my quantities, but it worked. The baby took it as if it were elixir and fell asleep in my arms as the last drop squelched out of the bottle. I put him over my shoulder and patted him as I had seen my wife do, and that worked as well. All we had to do now was to park him and have something to eat ourselves.

The lounge of the hotel was furnished with bucket chairs in bright red leather. Two of them together made a natural cradle. Ruth lined them with shawls and was just lowering the baby into them when the manager turned up again.
"Ah! – monsieur, Non!"

Pour quoi non?" I said.

"Et alors! If the baby becomes. …damp, what will happen to the colour of my chairs?"

"This is Christmas," I said, "a time for babies, not for colours."

As he opened his mouth to argue, a melody of bells drifted, sharp and soft across the city.

"What's that?" I said.

"That, monsieur, that is …… Bon Noel," he smiled.

"Oh, Merry Christmas," I said.

We looked at Ruth; she put the baby into the chairs. "Shalom." She said.

Which is, after all, the word He might have used Himself.

THE FACE BEHIND THE WHISKERS

Christmas is a nostalgic time, isn't it? You always start thinking about other Christmases. A few years ago I was working on the last picture scheduled to be made at one of the biggest film studios in England. A 'chippy' I was, working under Charlie Plaistowe, one of the best carpenters in the business.

And I'll never forget the look on his face that Friday when he came into the shop after the weekly meeting up at the production office and said "This is it boys. "Flaming Lady" finishes shooting next Wednesday, Carpenters' Shop Staff collect their chips and cards next Friday."

"Flash! Chippies get chips" shouted one of the bright boys. "Ouch!!" he cried, as I dropped a fourteen-inch plane on his foot.

I knew what it meant to Charlie. Fifteen years he'd been knocking around in the business and four years ago he'd married Jeannie, from the script department. Now there was Gillian as well, a lovely little kid, just past her third birthday. And there we all were with Christmas coming up in a couple of months and not much else in view, with the film business collapsing all around us like a set of leaky bagpipes.

When Charlie told Jeannie about it she wasn't that worried. After all, there's always plenty of work for a skilled craftsman.

But she'd reckoned without Charlie's attitude to his job. Working in the film business he'd always felt a bit different; part of something.... creative. There's a special sort of feeling that people working in the entertainment line get: chippies, sparks, chorus girls, stars; all of them. And they're just plain useless at anything else until they get it out of their system; and that isn't easy when your system's been running that way as long as Charlie's had.

The first couple of weeks when he came back from the labour exchange, Jeannie didn't say anything when he told her that there was nothing doing. In a way, it was fun, being on holiday when everybody else was hard at it.

But the third week she told him straight that Christmas was coming and the purse was getting thin. He tried to explain the way that he felt but all that Jeannie said was that she felt houses were just as creative as film sets - and a sight more practical; to say nothing of ships, shops and factories.

The next week, after breakfast, as he was going to sign on, they started the same argument again and she let her hair down properly. "You and your 'creative' work," she said, "Who do you think you are, Salvador Dali?"

"He's only a painter!" shouted Charlie.

"Anyway, he earns a living!" she shouted back. "I bet his kids have turkey and Christmas pudding. And Gillian wants a tricycle."

Charlie could see that the argument was getting a bit silly, so he tried a more reasonable line: "Look love," he said, "suppose I take any old job they serve up to me, and then the studio calls, if I'm out there shovelling snow, and I'm stuck with it for week, I'll miss the job."

"Studio call!" she said, "The only call you'll get from there will be a black-edged invitation to the funeral of the British Film Industry. I warn you Charlie Plaistowe, either you change your ideas or I'll leave you and go out to work myself."

"Don't talk silly," he said, "What would happen to Gillian?"

"I'll put her in Mr Reed's home," she said, "At least she'll get a decent Christmas there!

"That's enough of that," said Charlie, "I don't want to hear any more of that nonsense. And I'll take a job when they offer me one that suits me, and not before. Understand?" And with that he stormed out of their two rooms, kitchen and bath.

By the time that he got to the labour exchange he'd simmered down of course, and when the little man behind the grille said "Ah, Mr Plaistowe, I think I've got something in your line." Well, his heart got in the way of his tonsils, and he could hardly ask what it was. "You're in the entertainment line, aren't you?" said the little man.

"Yes," Said Charlie. "Have the studios re-opened?"

"Studios?" said the little man, "uh, ...no."

"Somebody want a stage carpenter for a Panto.?" asked Charlie.

"No. ....No." said the dole bloke. "It's Everington's; you know, the big store in the high street. They want someone to be Santa Claus in their toy department ...."

"Santa Claus!" said Charlie, "What's that got to do with the entertainment business?"

"Well," he said, "you know, dressing up and whiskers and all that."

"What do you take me for?" Spluttered Charlie. "I'm a carpenter. I ...."

"Oh, I didn't mean to .... I only thought .... you see ....."

"All right," said Charlie "I'll take it." And he took the card the little man was holding. "Now perhaps she'll be satisfied," he said.

"Oh," said the little man, "Yes, well, I most certainly hope ...." and Charlie left him twittering behind his wire, like a budgerigar that's just been stroked by a tom-cat.

Well, he went over to Everington's, tried on the red coat and whiskers and clinched the job with the manager, to start at 8 o'clock the next morning.

Then he went home. There was a sort of hollow sound to the front door when slammed it and when he got into his own flat he could only hear himself and he knew, before he opened a door, that the rooms were empty and he began to feel scared when he saw that Jeannie's dressing gown was gone from the peg behind the bedroom door. He rushed into Gillian's room and the drawers of the little chest he had made for her were hanging open and were empty - like a box full of empty yawns. 'Mr Reeds' he thought. 'She said she'd take her to Mr Reed's' and he tore out of the flat again.

Mr Reed was a big, serious man, with a twinkle. He ran the local children's home and that seemed to cover all sorts - children whose parent were dead; children whose parents weren't fit to keep them; children whose parents couldn't keep them - all sorts. Charlie and Jean had met him at whist drives and jumble sales and local charity do's. He seemed to be expecting Charlie: "Hello, Mr Plaistowe," he said.

"Is Gillian here?" asked Charlie.

"Yes," replied Mr Reed.

"I want her." Said Charlie.

"Of course. I'll send for her." He said. "Is her mother with you?"

"No" said Charlie, "I don't know where she is."

Mr Reed took his finger away from the bell, without pushing it. "You mean at this moment?" he said.

"This moment or any other moment," said Charlie.

"You mean she's not at home to look after Gillian?" enquired Mr Reed.

"I'm capable of looking after her, aren't I?" Said Charlie.

"Are you working, Mr Plaistowe?" asked Mr Reed.

"If you think I can't support her, you're wrong," said Charlie, I'm starting a new job tomorrow - and you can tell that to my wife the next time she comes!"

"Do you propose taking Gillian to work with you?" Asked Mr Reed.

"Of course not," said Charlie, I ...."

"Then you intend that she shall be left alone in your rooms all day?"

"Well, I...."

"No, Mr Plaistowe," said Reed. "Surely, in your heart you agree that for the time being Gillian is better off here? At least until we hear from your wife."

Charlie knew he was talking sense, and didn't say any more.

Jeannie didn't come home that night, and when Charlie got all dolled up in Everington's toy department, next morning, you'd have thought, to look at him, that Santa Claus' reindeer had broken a leg and he'd had to walk the last hundred miles all through the night.

The manager noticed it too. "We must smile and be jolly, mustn't we?" he said

"Must we?" said Charlie.

"Joyous! Effulgent!" said the manager. "Season of festive merriment. Let us be radiant."

"Bit early yet ain't it?" said Charlie.

"HaHa! Jester." bubbled the manager, and whipped off, spreading joy throughout the department, like a sprig of mistletoe in a home for aged bachelors.

Well Charlie nearly put his foot in it with his first customer: a very fat little boy kicked him on the ankle to attract his attention, held out a 10p piece and said "I want one of them." pointing to a £5. set of railway lines.

"Oh do you?" said Charlie, rubbing his ankle, "Well you can't have one. They cost a fiver, not 10p. Who do you think I am, Santa Claus?"

"Of course you're Santa Claus, young man!" Said the manager, as the boy's mother came forward with £5.

"Oh yes," said Charlie. "Of course."

Still, he struggled along through the rest of the day; a day full of other people's happy faces and other people's happy children, and he might have stuck the job out all right if it hadn't been for a party of kids that came in the late afternoon. Twenty of them, just being taken round to see the bright colours of Christmas. They were the kids from Mr Reed's home, and there, in the middle of them, was Gillian. Well, that was too much for Charlie.

"Walk up, Walk up!" he shouted, and the party came streaming over with their escort fussing behind them like a mother hen with her chicks. "What would you like from Santa Claus?" Charlie asked the first little girl. "That dolly, please," she said, pointing, and he gave it to her.

"I'm afraid it's a misunderstanding" fussed the mother hen,

"Don't you believe in Santa Claus, Missus?" said Charlie

"Well," she stuttered, looking round at the children, "of course I do, but...."

"Well" said Charlie, "I'm him". and he kept on dishing out the presents until he came to Gillian. "Well love" he said, "What would you like?"

"I don't want nothing" she said.

"Now, now," he said, "surely there's something you want for Christmas?"

"I want my mummy and Daddy" she said, and started to cry.

But before Charlie could do anything, up came the manager with blood pressure and a policeman. "There he is constable. Heaven knows how much stock he has stolen."

"I didn't steal it," said Charlie, "I gave it away."

"It wasn't yours to give away!" said the manager. "Please remove him constable. I'll come to the station later to press charges."

"You'd better come along chum," said the copper.

Charlie stripped of the robes and had just got to the beard and moustache, when he saw Gillian watching him. "Do you mind if I keep the whiskers on mate?" he muttered.

"Eh?" said the policeman. He looked at Charlie then he looked at the kids. "Oh," he said quietly "I thought they were natural. All the same" he said, looking round for the manager, we'd better get weaving before Phil the Fluter gets back."

"Thanks" said Charlie.

That was Charlie's first night behind bars, and he didn't like it. He still wasn't liking it when they took him out to the sergeant's desk first thing the next morning, and there was the manager of the toy department waiting for him.

"Well, well, Mr Plaistowe" he said, "all is forgiven and forgotten."

"Eh?" said Charlie.

"Let us hear no more of the whole affair."

"What?!" said Charlie.

"I think he means that they're withdrawing charges." Said the Sergeant.

"Why?" said Charlie.

"Well," said the manager, "season of good will and mellow fruitfulness."

"Where was the good will last night?" asked Charlie. "Come on, something's made you change your mind."

"Well," said the manager, "We've had some excellent publicity as the result of your behaviour. We've even had a film company on the 'phone, asking for details. They propose to make a film based on the incident. So, all is forgiven and your position awaits you."

"You must be joking," said Charlie, "once in that position is quite enough, thank you. I'm going home for a bath and a decent sleep."

He was about half-way up the stairs to the flat when he smelt bacon frying. It got stronger as he got nearer, and when he opened the door he could *hear* frying as well. He walked into the kitchen:

"Hello," said Jeannie, "Where were you last night?"

"Never you mind." he said, hoping that she wouldn't notice how glad he was that she didn't know. "Where were you the night before?"

"I went back to mum's of course."

"Well why didn't you take Gillian?"

"Because when I left here I didn't know that I was going back to mum's."

"Oh," said Charlie. And thought he'd better leave it at that.

"She's in the other room if you want to see her," said Jean, "and you haven't kissed me good morning yet."

Charlie didn't move.

"Oh all right sulky." She said. "By the way, the studio called."

"The studio!" said Charlie, "Well come on, what did they want?"

"They want you for a film."

"What film?"

"A quickie they're making - something about a chap who works in a store as Santa Claus and gives the presents away instead of selling them."

"You're joking," said Charlie.

"It does sound silly, doesn't it?" she said, "but they want you all right."

"What do they want me for?" said Charlie slowly.

"What for?" she said. "Chippy of course. Do you think they want you to play Santa Claus? You wouldn't even know what he looks like!"

"No," said Charlie, "But I could learn, couldn't I?" And then he kissed her.

<u>ACKNOWLEDGEMENTS.</u>

My thanks to Muriel Hague for her charming illustrations and Jonathan Miller for his help and guidance.

Lightning Source UK Ltd.
Milton Keynes UK
10 November 2009

146063UK00001B/8/P